A Candlelight Ecstasy Romance™

HE TOOK FULL ADVANTAGE OF HER INSTINCTIVE GASP OF OUTRAGE. . . .

His mouth closed over hers and ruthlessly plundered every sweet corner. Their mouths became a fiery seal, welding them together for a timeless instant, lasting as long as infinity, and as short as the beat of a heart. When Dain lifted his mouth from hers, Keri wasn't sure she'd ever be able to draw breath again without recalling the taste of his lips.

He laid his free hand against the side of her neck and said softly, "If I had more time . . ." and left her standing there bemused, in the middle of his office, the carefully typed envelopes and letters in a scattered drift around her feet.

CANDLELIGHT ECSTASY ROMANCES™

DECEPTIVE LOVE

Anne N. Reisser

A CANDLELIGHT ECSTASY ROMANCE™

Published by
Dell Publishing Co., Inc.
1 Dag Hammarskjold Plaza
New York, New York 10017

Dell ® TM 681510, Dell Publishing Co., Inc.

Candlelight Ecstasy Romance™ is a trademark of
Dell Publishing Co., Inc., New York, New York.

ISBN: 0-440-11776-3

Printed in the United States of America

First printing—December 1981

Dear Reader:

In response to your enthusiasm for Candlelight Ecstasy Romances™, we are now increasing the number of titles per month from two to three.

We are pleased to offer you sensuous novels set in America, depicting modern American women and men as they confront the provocative problems of a modern relationship.

Throughout the history of the Candlelight line, Dell has tried to maintain a high standard of excellence, to give you the finest in reading pleasure. It is now and will remain our most ardent ambition.

Vivian Stephens
Editor
Candlelight Romances

DECEPTIVE LOVE

CHAPTER 1

The phone shrilled insistently. He knocked his hand painfully against the nightstand, fumbling in the dark to cut off its shattering summons.

"You've got to come home! That girl is wrecking my life!"

The newly wakened man ran a weary hand over his stubbly chin and squinted at the luminous dial of the wristwatch lying by the phone. He dropped his head back on the pillow, mouthing a silent curse. It was three A.M. and he'd been in his bed for little more than an hour. Thinking comes hard in those circumstances, especially when the woman on the other end of the phone is hysterical and an ocean and part of a continent away.

"Calm down, Denise," he advised with commendable forbearance. "Who is *she* and what's *she* done to your life specifically?"

"She's trying to take Schyler away from me, that's what! I want you to fire her and make sure she never gets work again." An acid hatred coated each word as it spat from the phone. Denise had had more than one drink, and alcohol made her vicious.

"Who the hell is Schyler?"

"He's my fiancé and we've only been engaged two weeks. Now he wants to break the engagement because of that tramp. Dain, you've just got to do *something!*" It was a familiar demand, punctuated by hiccuping sobs, also familiar. He closed his eyes on the darkness of his room in exasperation.

"Schyler who, Denise?" he questioned patiently. He knew only patience could extract coherence from his mercurial sister in this mood. "How long have you known him? I've only been gone four months and this is the first I've heard of a Schyler, much less one who's engaged to my sister." He was holding on to his temper with both hands. At her most rational Denise was trying. Hysterical she was impossible.

"Schyler Van Metre, of *the* Van Metres . . . you know . . . Van Metre and Company and all of that." He could just picture her vague, encompassing gesture. "I met him two months ago—at a party. He *just* gave me the most gorgeous diamond engagement ring and now he says that since he's found this woman again he can't marry me." A pleading note, well-practiced and cajoling, entered her voice. "I want him, Dain. She works for you, so *you* get rid of her. That's where he saw her again, so it's all your fault."

Ignoring the magnificent irrationality of this statement, he asked reasonably, "All right, next question: who is *she?*"

"Her name is Keri Dalton and what he sees in her is beyond me" was the enlightening answer.

10

"I don't know any Keri Dalton, Denise," he responded with ebbing patience. "Are you sure she works for me? All right, all right. So she was hired three months ago." He broke through the babble of sound ruthlessly. "I'll be home in a few days," he promised wearily. "I'll see what I can do then. Good night, Denise." He dropped the receiver back onto its rest, cutting off the further spate of words in mid-flow.

Dain Randolph is coming back. Word flew through the office grapevine with the speed and degree of accuracy of all such organs. It was served as speculation with the morning coffee rolls and as established fact over the lunch hot-plate special. It meant less than nothing to Keri. No premonitory chill ghosted over her skin. No misgiving prickled the hairs at the nape of her neck as she worked composedly at her desk.

To the office staff she was the efficient Miss Dalton, of impeccable qualifications and calm impersonality. She could have been an employee of long years' seniority, so smoothly and unobtrusively had she carved her new niche. Keri had chosen her job well and had great hopes of at last being able to settle down.

George Simonds, her new boss, was in his mid-fifties and dotingly in love with his motherly wife. He saw Keri purely as the formidable Miss Dalton and never delved into her personal life. Mr. Simonds and Keri had no social discourse, except for the perfunctory "Good morning, Miss Dalton. How are you today?" to which she invariably replied, "Fine, thank you, Mr. Simonds. Your mail is waiting for you on your desk." Keri had set the tone firmly on her first day at work and had allowed no deviation during her three months at RanCo. She intended to allow none.

When Keri had found it necessary to quit her fourth job, in New York, six months before, she had ruefully decided that only drastic measures were going to suffice if she ever hoped to hold a job for any appreciable length of time.

Keri was honest with herself. She wouldn't want to be *ugly,* but she was more than just a body. She deeply resent-ed the masculine assumption that a nicely curved body indicated a willing libido, especially when that assumption slipped over into her working life. Being a man's secretary did not also indicate a willingness to be his bed partner!

So she decided: If the men she worked for could not or would not leave her alone, she would henceforth make sure that they saw nothing worthwhile, from a masculine standpoint, to distract them during business hours. She would keep her business and private lives totally separate.

She hid her emerald green eyes behind clear-lensed horn-rimmed glasses and ruthlessly subdued her glorious titian hair in a tight French twist. Her lush figure, the source of much of her problem, disappeared under severe-ly tailored suits of uncompromising primness and drab coloring. There wasn't much she could do about the shapely perfection of her long, slender legs except wear "sensible" shoes.

Instead of making up, she made down. She used a light-er than normal lipstick to de-emphasize the full lower lip and curved upper lip of her cleanly modeled mouth and the outsized horned-rims overwhelmed the classic nose and high cheekbones. A dusting of sallow powder did the rest, destroying the effect of her flawless skin.

"disguise" complete she was subtly aged to a colorless, indeterminate "over-30."

Even her voice at the office bore little resemblance to the husky contralto of her normal usage. She had adopted a brisk, no-nonsense intonation which was polite but chill in its precision. She was a dragon of the most formidable, with a breath of ice rather than fire.

As a masquerade it had proved satisfactory and efficacious, but she had thought it all for naught one day last week when Schyler strolled past her in the hall. She had tensed, braced for exposure, but he showed no flicker of recognition on that handsome, petulant face. She had forced her legs to continue their measured pace down the long corridor until she reached the sanctuary of her office.

She had dropped the papers she carried in a scattered drift atop her desk and slumped into her chair. Senseless to feel so shaky, to let the sight of a man she had hoped never to see again unnerve her so badly, but he had marked the final link in an unpleasant chain of experiences.

Schyler Van Metre, scion of Van Metre and Company. Down that corridor strode her reason for retreat into protective camouflage, but it would seem, she assured herself hopefully, that he was also a testament to its effectiveness.

She had worked for his father, executive secretary to the chairman of the board of Van Metre and Company, until father and son, between them, made it impossible for her to continue. The son had pursued her ruthlessly and the father had tried to buy her for his son. If she *never* heard the name again, it would be too soon! But Keri had what she wanted now—a boss who didn't see her as a woman and a pleasantly active social life totally separate from her

13

business persona. She had the best of both worlds and she intended to *keep* them.

Now, a week after her nerve-twisting confrontation, she could relax. There were evidently to be no repercussions, no word from Schyler, and best of all, no further sight of him. He had disappeared from the corridors of RanCo as mysteriously as he had appeared.

She covered her typewriter and gathered her purse with a thankful sigh. She enjoyed her work, but it was always a relief to go home and shed her dowdy image.

"Good night, Miss Dalton. Have a pleasant weekend."

"Thank you, Mr. Simonds." Keri turned away so that Mr. Simonds couldn't see the mischievous smile which she was unable to restrain. Probably thinks I'm going home to my lonely apartment and my tabby cat! Maybe I should bring a basket of some anonymous gray knitting to work with me every once in a while, to reinforce the image. When she turned back she had schooled her errant expression and was able to present him with a demure nod before preceding him to the parking lot where her car awaited her, crouched like a dangerous, snarling, jungle beast, ready to roar to powerful life at the touch of her hand on the key.

Eyebrows were always raised when she drove out of the company parking lot, but she had balked at extending her masquerade to her beloved car. The sight of the prim Miss Dalton expertly guiding her dark green Porsche among the staid Fords and Chevrolets was an anomalous sight. She had gotten it two years ago when her parents had left for a new assignment abroad.

Her father was an officer in the army and had recently received his second star. Keri had grown up feeling at home all over the world, with a flair for languages en-

14

couraged by multinationaled playmates. She spoke French and German flawlessly, Italian and Spanish fluently, and Japanese understandably. She was familiar with many of the world's capitals and was an accomplished hostess. Rank did not awe her. Her godfather was a distinguished retired ambassador, still consulted for his expertise and shrewd analysis of political complexities. She had friends in high places and she breathed easily in rarefied air.

Some day she might wish to travel again, in which event she would easily find a post abroad . . . her qualifications would see to that . . . but for now she wanted a permanent home. That had been one of the more distressing aspects of Schyler's relentless pursuit.

She had left her previous job, and had been lured to Van Metre and Company by an exorbitant salary offer from Van Metre, Sr., because of her extraordinary qualifications. She quickly became indispensable to Carleton Van Metre, who was a bit of a snob, but overall a good boss. He also appreciated the fact that his secretary combined a cool intelligence with a stunningly lovely appearance. He *did not* enjoy the fact that his son had begun a determined effort to seduce his new secretary from the moment he laid eyes upon her.

Keri didn't enjoy the fact either! Schyler had interfered with her work, hounded her at home, and generally made a miserable nuisance of himself. He was superficially handsome, but Keri quickly found him to be weak and self-indulgent as well. He was not a man she could either trust or respect—a death knell for any hopes he might have cherished of arousing her deeper interest and emotions. As the daughter of an officer whose assignments had taken him to embassy posts all over the world, she

15

was well inoculated against the sophisticated charm which said so much and meant so little.

She had made the intitial error, she admitted to herself wryly, in accepting dates with him on a casual basis, but he had quickly made it clear that he wished to move from the casual to the intimate with all possible speed. She refused to go out with him anymore, but he developed the disconcerting habit of appearing at her front door with no warning, or perching on her desk while she was trying to transcribe dictation from his father. Another woman might have found it flattering but Keri found it just tiresome and then actively distressing. Schyler could not, would never, be her choice of mate, and she was not a girl for a casual fling, no matter how glittering the opportunity.

She remonstrated, she fumed, she ignored. The climax came when he asked her to marry him, which she refused to do. He was astounded, disbelieving. No girl in her right mind would turn down Schyler Van Metre of *the* Van Metres. He had been pursued by women since puberty, for himself and for what he had, and he'd gotten everything he wanted from them all. Now, when he wanted marriage, it was simply inconceivable that she deny him!

It was inconceivable to his father as well. She was only a secretary! How could she deny a Van Metre when he condescended to honor her? This attitude caused Keri to mutter, sotto voice, that the days of *droit de seigneur* were long since dead, a sentiment she didn't utter aloud at first because she still hoped to stay at her job. Schyler's father saw her as an asset—a beautiful brood mare, a gracious hostess, and a serf properly appreciative of the honor done her. Keri endured some weeks of mental bludgeoning,

16

gave her notice, trained her successor in stony silence, and left.

Her action freed her from Van Metre, Sr., but Schyler was made of more persistent fiber. He phoned, he appeared, he dogged her footsteps. He promised that he would continue to do so until she gave in out of sheer exhaustion. Keri was unwillingly forced to believe him. The Schyler she knew through gossip and observation was not this determined, obsessed man.

Keri closed her apartment, called her father's sister to warn her of an impending visitor, and left town. She had plenty of savings, and when she sought another job, it wouldn't be in New York, where she was likely to run across *the* Van Metres again, any of them!

After several months of enjoyable idleness at her aunt's beachside cottage, Keri decided it was time to go back to work. She was determined to leave no ties with the Van Metres unsevered, so, for the first time in her life, she used the friendship and influence of her godfather for her benefit. She explained the situation to him and emphasized the reason for her unwillingness to obtain a reference from her former employer. If Schyler knew she had contacted his father for a reference, he might seek and *find* her again.

Her godfather understood "all too well," he advised her with a twinkle in his eyes. "You've been beating them off with a stick from your crib days, Keri."

"Well, I won't have to at work anymore," she retorted tartly. "I have a *plan.*"

She told him of her proposed transformation and he chuckled deeply. "Some smart man is going to see through to the real you without half trying, my dear. You can't hide that redheaded light under a bushel indefinitely."

"Charles! My hair is not red," she remonstrated, carry

17

ing on a familiar, teasing argument between them. "Anyway," she pointed out, "it will make the job interview much easier. No one believes I can do what I say I can. It's time to look the part."

"Did you have problems at your previous jobs, before Van Metre, I mean?" he asked her curiously.

"To a certain extent," she admitted a bit unwillingly. "Not to the degree of nuisance value that Schyler has managed to attain, but annoying all the same. The old jokes about bosses chasing their secretaries around the desk don't sound so funny when you have your track shoes on. From now on I'm going to keep my private life strictly private. *Absolutely* no dates with anyone I work with, or for! Charles, I want a boss who's happily married and at least fifty, and he has to be someone who will take me on your personal recommendation so I don't have to explain Van Metre and Company. I don't expect the same level of salary that I got from Van Metre . . . that would be hard to match . . . but I don't mind working the same field."

"A vice-president or better, eh?" he smiled. "Fortunately, just the man springs to mind. His secretary of fifteen years recently surprised everyone by marrying a widower with four small children, and he's desperate. You'll be a pleasant surprise for him, and I can guarantee that he's never looked at another woman since he married his wife thirty years ago."

"Made to order. Bless you, Charles." Keri dropped a kiss on his bald spot. "I really know how to pick godfathers," she finished smugly.

He laughed.

So she had come to work for George Simonds and found him exactly tailored to her needs. She had had that moment of panic when she passed Schyler in the hall, but it had been nearly a week ago and if he'd recognized her, she would certainly have found him on her doorstep before now.

All of these reflections faded from Keri's mind as the traffic jam she was trapped in finally began to break up. She gunned the Porsche through an opening which left several other drivers muttering about "women drivers" even while admiring the cool expertise which had freed her, like a cork popping out of a bottle, from the snaking line of cars.

She parked the car in its assigned bay in the underground garage attached to her apartment building. Then, while the elevator carried her swiftly to her floor, she freed her shoulder-length hair from its cruelly tight confinement. She shook her head to loose and fluff her hair until it swirled in comfortable disorder around her face. She shed her suit jacket, unbuttoned the first two buttons of her drab tan blouse, and stretched. She felt like a snake that had just shed a too-tight skin; for a weekend at least, she reminded herself.

She stepped out of the elevator when it reached her floor and stopped dead in shock.

"Hello, Miss Prim. Long time no see." The lounging man raked an appraising eye up and down her length and smiled slightly. "I'm glad to see that the transformation is only skin deep and not meant to be permanent."

"Schyler!" she gasped. "How . . . how did you find me? What are you doing here? *Oh, go away!*" It was practically a wail. Keri could have stamped her feet in a tantrum.

"Did you think I wouldn't recognize you, Keri?" Schyler asked with simulated surprise. "I know every line of that lovely body of yours and I'd recognize you draped in a grain sack with a paper bag over your head. You'd do

19

well to change your walk as well, my dear, when you try to disguise yourself," he advised helpfully. "Any man with a normal hormone level could spot you by your walk alone, not to mention those lovely legs."

She looked at him with dislike. He was still the same cocksure gallant, convinced no woman could resist him in the end. Was it all to start again? Well, this time she would not run. He had no hold, no lever to use. She put her key into the door of her apartment, opened it, and stepped inside. She started to close the door, but Schyler put his foot in the way. Keri glanced down at the shining shoe firmly planted over her threshold and then back up to his face, her own face expressionless, patient.

"Aren't you going to ask me in, Keri darling?" he smiled engagingly.

"No," she stated positively. "We have nothing to say to each other, Schyler. I won't marry you. I won't have an affair with you, and I won't go out with you." She tried to close the door again.

"Comprehensive." He seemed unmoved by her vehemence. "Let me in, Keri, just for a drink. I promise I'll go when you tell me, but I'd like to talk to you. I haven't seen you for six months." He grinned with wheedling good humor. "I don't count that little meeting in the halls of RanCo. That wasn't the real you. I nearly burst out laughing, you know, when you passed by us. Lord, what a sight! Halloween came early this year."

In spite of her annoyance, Keri couldn't resist a small grin. He had a slick charm when he chose to use it. "But very effective," she assured him. "I haven't had any distractions while I'm trying to get my work done. It makes for a most restful atmosphere. I wish I'd thought of it sooner."

20

His foot hadn't retreated an inch. She sighed resignedly and gave in with marked lack of enthusiasm, saying ungraciously, "All right, Schyler. Come in. Just one drink though, and then out you go. I have a date for dinner and a party."

He scowled. "I told you any man could see through that ridiculous masquerade. Who is he?"

He trailed her into the living room as he spoke and she glared back over her shoulder at him. "None of your business, Schyler," she emphasized tightly. "I'll tell you this, though. He *doesn't* have any connection with RanCo. I'll never again make the mistake of going out with someone I work with or for. You cured me of that quite thoroughly and lost me an excellent job in the process. Now I keep my business and personal lives entirely separate and it works very nicely, thank you."

She tossed the suit jacket and her purse onto a nearby armchair and walked into a small kitchen, hidden behind slatted wooden doors. He heard ice cubes clink into a glass, followed almost immediately by the gurgle of a liquid. She came back into the living room and thrust a glass at him. "Scotch."

"You remembered, darling. A sign of affection at last." He was still standing in the middle of her living room and he looked around with interest. "Very nice. May I sit, Keri, or must I gulp my scotch down while you stand glaring at me?"

Once again that whimsical note disarmed her and she gestured, exasperated, toward the dark-blue tweed couch. He promptly sat in the middle of the couch and patted the cushion beside him invitingly.

She snorted and shook her head emphatically. "No, Schyler. No, no, and no again! Isn't that word in your

21

vocabulary at all? Go find yourself another girl and leave me to get on with my life in my own way."

"There are plenty of girls, women too, for that matter," he admitted. "They're easy to find." His mouth had an odd twist to it. "I know that all too well, Keri, my love, but there's only one Keri Dalton of the glorious hair and green eyes. I thought I could be content with less, but now that I've found you once more, I know I won't let you go again."

It was only with the greatest exercise of will that Keri kept from pounding her head against the nearest wall. "What does it take to convince you, Schyler? I *don't* love you, I *don't* want to marry you! I can't make it any plainer than that."

"Are you in love with someone else, Keri? Tell me honestly that you are and I might believe you." He watched her closely.

She tried to evade his questions. "What difference does it make, if I'm not in love with *you?* Schyler, please believe me, there's no future in this . . . this pursuit."

"If you don't love someone else, you might as well love me," he said outrageously. "I'm young, not bad looking, rich, and I've been told I make love rather nicely. Take me on approval, Keri. I wear well."

"Incorrigible, impossible, and insane. Finish your drink, Schyler, and go away. I want to get ready for my date." When he showed no immediate signs of leaving, she reminded him, "You promised you'd go when I told you to."

To her unexpressed but pleased surprise he rose obediently and prepared to leave. She hadn't decided on a course of action should he refuse, except perhaps to call David. David lived in an apartment two floors above her.

22

They had met several months ago at the elevator, she going to the laundry area and he coming from it, balancing an untidy pile of freshly dried clothes. He promptly followed her, to make conversation and fold his clothes while hers washed and dried.

David was an amiable bear of a man and big enough to shift Schyler, but she shrank from that expedient unless absolutely necessary. It wasn't to her taste to have men fighting over her, and it might also give David ideas about his proprietary rights which she would prefer not to have raised. She and David had a most pleasant relationship and she had no desire to pass beyond the casual good-night-kiss stage with him for the nonce. He was one of several men she dated companionably. It wouldn't suit her to single him out, except in desperation.

"All right, Keri. I did promise. Your wish is my command, with the exception, of course, of your wish for me to go out of your life. You might as well get used to the fact that I'm not going to do that." There was a note of grim determination in his voice, a warning she would do well not to disregard.

When he had gone she carried his glass, with its melting ice cubes and residue of diluted scotch, to the kitchen and dumped the remains down the kitchen sink. She really didn't understand Schyler at all. He had been a lighthearted playboy, happily flitting from feminine blossom to feminine blossom, to the despair of Van Metre, Sr., who had a strong dynastic sense. Schyler was the last of the Van Metre males, although he had several sisters, and it would be unthinkable to break the chain of direct descent from the founding Van Metre who had set up the family fortunes in the mid-eighteenth century by means better not enquired into too closely.

23

The Schyler of merely a year ago had blithely resisted all his father's persuasions and strictures on marriage, hence a partial explanation of Van Metre, Sr.'s initial delight and then astounded dismay at the course of his son's courtship of Keri.

Schyler had played at love too often and too long, Keri judged. She didn't want a man who was, at heart, every woman's man. He wanted her, would even marry her, because she was unattainable, but once he had her, another flower would eventually beckon and away he'd flit. She was of no mind to share her man once she had accepted him as hers, and as yet she'd met no man she had had the slightest desire to claim. One thing was certain, however. It wouldn't be Schyler!

She saw neither hide nor hair of Schyler for the rest of the weekend, although a charming nosegay of flowers arrived early Saturday morning. There was a card bearing a single, flamboyant *S* attached and she shook her head dolefully. She didn't dump them in the wastebasket because she didn't believe in wasted gestures. It wasn't the flowers' fault, but had Schyler been present to witness the action, she would have consigned them to the trash with emphatic force.

Monday morning was typical of such days. She snagged two pairs of nonrunnable panty hose and broke a fingernail before the day had fairly begun. When she finally reached the office, she was as close to being late as she'd ever been in her working life and she hoped it didn't foretell a day spent accomplishing things by the skin of her teeth.

Her weekend had not been the relaxed one she had planned. She had been eternally tensed for Schyler's ap-

24

pearance, making it impossible for her to fully enjoy the party or the play the following evening. Sunday she had spent with Charles and Mary, lounging by their pool, but even Charles had little solace to offer when she told him of Schyler's reappearance in her life. Mary, who was a dear, thought it romantic. Keri assured her that it came closer to being a grade-one nuisance, but made little impression on Mary's opinion.

Keri managed to open and sort Mr. Simonds's mail before he came in, prepared to carry out her portion of their daily routine, but still with that sense of having to run just to keep in place. Mr. Simonds swept into the office with an unusual air of fluster himself, and before she could open her mouth to respond to his invariable greeting, he snapped out, "Come into my office, please, Miss Dalton," and bustled right past her into his own office.

"Well, well!" Keri's eyebrows rose in astonishment. "Someone's really been upsetting his routine." Mr. Simonds was a nice man, but he did tend to be persnickity. He did not like change. Keri gathered up her dictation pad, ready to take down a blistering letter or memo to the offender, and followed him into the office.

He swept his morning mail aside with a petulant gesture quite foreign to his usual manner. Keri sat in her customary chair, pencil poised, expression attentive.

"Mr. Randolph's back." The words were abrupt. Keri eyed her boss with some speculation, but responded with a noncommittal murmur. "He wasn't due back for another month," Mr. Simonds added plaintively. Keri maintained her attentive expression, but inwardly her eyebrows were raised to her hairline!

She knew nothing of Mr. Randolph save his scrawled initials, D.R., which adorned countless memos, letters, and figure-packed papers which she filed, routed, and duplicated as required. He was RanCo, and he had been in Geneva, Paris, London, Rome, and various other major cities ever since she had come to work for Mr. Simonds, and through him, RanCo. Mr. Simonds was a vice-president (as specified to Charles). D. Randolph was the major stockholder in the family-held corporation and the power on the throne. Judging from his output, he was also a workoholic.

Had she felt so inclined, she could have found out everything about him from his shoe size to the name of his first-grade teacher. An office grapevine is thorough, if not always accurate. But Keri hadn't been inclined. She knew the *D* stood for Dain. She wouldn't recognize him if she passed him in the hall.

If she had thought about the matter, cared enough to try to visualize the man, she would have pictured him as dynamic, bull-necked, and cigar-chomping, held together by Maalox and high-blood pressure pills. His wife would be occupied with suitable charities and the Opera Committee and his children would be stashed away in various Ivy League schools. But she hadn't cared enough to even speculate.

"Do you really speak all the languages Charles told me?" Mr. Simonds sounded hopeful that it had been sheer fabrication on Charles's part.

Keri looked at her boss in surprise. "Of course, sir," she answered stiffly. "Mr. Lawson wouldn't have said so if I could not. I do not, however, read Japanese, but I believe he made that clear, did he not?"

"Hmm, yes, yes," Mr. Simonds admitted abstractedly, "but you won't need the Japanese. The German and

French are the necessary ones, although the Italian could be useful as well."

"Useful, sir?" Keri was by now thoroughly bewildered. She had known this was going to be a strange day, but she hadn't realized it was going to affect everyone around her as well.

"Of course. I told you. Mr. Randolph is back." He leaned back in his chair, drumming his fingers impatiently on his disarranged mail. He sighed heavily. "I hate to lose you, Miss Dalton. You're an even better secretary than Miss Mason was."

Praise indeed, thought Keri wryly. She breathed deeply once, for control, and said carefully, "Mr. Simonds, if you could just be a little more specific. I . . . I gather that I am no longer to be your secretary and that it is in some way connected with Mr. Randolph's return and my linguistic abilities, but . . ." she gestured her bewilderment expressively.

"He's already got two secretaries," Mr. Simonds exhorted in aggrieved tones. "Why does he have to have mine as well? There must be other secretaries who speak all those languages. I don't like all these changes!" He shuffled through the once carefully sorted piles of mail, totally disordering them. Keri gritted her teeth.

"Who, Mr. Simonds? Who has two secretaries? Mr. Randolph?" Keri strove to maintain a calm, rational tone. Someone had to!

"Of course. That's just what I said. He's back and he's commandeered you because you speak all of those languages." Mr. Simonds glared at her as though she had committed some despicable crime.

"But I'm *your* secretary," Keri said helplessly. What a Monday!

"Not anymore," Mr. Simonds informed her glumly. "A typist from the secretarial pool is coming up to do the routine work and Personnel has been notified to replace you as soon as they possibly can."

"You mean that this is a permanent change?" Behind the clear-glass lenses Keri's green eyes began to emit dangerous sparks. She had hand-picked this boss. He was just what she had ordered, and it didn't suit her plans at all to be shunted around to some other, possibly less congenial (from her point of view) situation.

"Why, of course." Mr. Simonds stared at her in surprise. She didn't sound happy about it at all! Every secretary who worked for the company would give her eye teeth to be one of Dain Randolph's secretaries, and not just for the higher salary the position carried either. For the first time since she had come to work for him, he really looked at Keri. There was something about this woman . . . a proud lift to the jaw line, the smooth clean line of her throat . . . which he had never noticed before. Her hair now . . . he shook his head. Fanciful, that's what he was. All this change was upsetting.

There was a soft tap at the inner door. Keri rose from her chair, walked over, and opened it. One of the secretaries from the typing pool stood uncertainly waiting. Keri knew her slightly and decided she was competent for an interim period, though not up to the sustained pressure of the job. She smiled reassuringly at the girl, and then turned back to Mr. Simonds.

"All right, sir. I understand you had no choice." She walked over to his desk and picked up the disarranged stack of mail, saying dryly, "I'll re-sort these and explain the procedure to Miss Gossard at the same time. I'll also brief her on the more urgent items and the general office routine. When I feel that she is ready to take over, I will report to Mr. Randolph's secretary.

"You had two calls which are fairly urgent. The memo is on your desk and if you would return them while Miss Gossard and I go over your mail, we'll be done by the time you're ready to deal with it."

Keri carried the mail out briskly, majestically sweeping an awed Miss Gossard before her. Mr. Simonds considered her exit in a somewhat bemused fashion and said, just as she reached the door, "But Miss Dalton, Mr. Randolph expects you at once. His Miss Barth was most specific."

Keri paused and responded in repressive accents. "Mr. Simonds, if I were to leave before I made sure everything was running as smoothly as possible under the circumstances, I would be a most inefficient secretary. Presumably Mr. Randolph desires my services because I am efficient. I shall leave your office in good order. Was there anything else, sir?"

"No, no. Carry on, Miss Dalton." He subsided. When she had shut the door quietly between the two offices, he pursed his lips in a silent whistle. Miss Dalton was definitely displeased. It made him feel somewhat better. His own day was not the only one to suffer unpleasant disruptions and inconvenience. Miss Dalton was on her high horse and he'd just found out how quelling she could be, seated upon such a lofty mount.

Keri dealt efficiently with the mail (for the second time) and answered Miss Gossard's questions, but her mind was busy on other things. Of all the rotten luck! Schyler back and now a new boss to impress with her colorless efficiency. Well, there was no help for it, she sighed. She'd just have to come down heavy as a dedicated and desiccated secretary until she sized up her new boss. He'd be more of a challenge to work for—any man who could keep three secretaries busy had to be—but she wasn't worried about her ability to cope with any job. She just sent up a fervent prayer that this boss was devoted to his own wife as well.

Miss Gossard was watching Keri with wide eyes. The lucky girl, to be going to work for Dain Randolph! Not that she looked capable of utilizing her chances in *that* direction, though. A very icy customer, Miss Dalton, although if she did something about her clothes and hair, and maybe got contact lenses . . . why, she might even be passable.

Keri was blissfully unaware of Miss Gossard's speculations. She explained the filing system, briefed Miss Gossard on the current active contracts, told her how and when Mr. Simonds preferred his coffee, and generally tried to prepare her to assume a burden beyond her capabilities.

When she had done all she felt was possible in the short time at her disposal, Keri tapped on Mr. Simonds's door and took her leave. She assured the slightly apprehensive Miss Gossard that she would be available if serious difficulties should arise. There was nothing personal to clear from her desk, so Keri gathered up her purse, nodded to Miss Gossard, and left.

Before she sought out her new office, Keri made a quick foray to the rest room. She wanted to be sure her prim exterior was as flawless as makeup and expression could make it. She recaptured several stray wisps of hair, renewed her lipstick and powder, assumed a formal, austere expression, and sailed forth to present herself to Mr. Randolph's Miss Barth.

Miss Barth was a revelation. She was as determinedly glamorous as Keri was determinedly effacing. Keri was

30

gleeful. With such a charmer available, it would be easy to remain part of the office furniture. Any roving eyes would stop on Miss Barth.

Not a flicker of her inward jubilation moved the smooth mask of her face. "I am Miss Dalton. I was told to report to you, Miss Barth. I understand that Mr. Randolph has requested my secretarial services." *There,* she thought with an inner smirk. *If that little speech doesn't establish me as a prig, nothing will.*

Miss Barth was obviously convinced. In her own way she was as pleased by Keri's appearance as Keri had been by hers. She cherished hopes, as yet totally unrealized, of becoming more than a secretary to Dain Randolph. She would not want to find another rival so near at hand. Mrs. Covey, the other secretary, was fair, fat, and fifty, a hand-me-down from Mr. Randolph's father.

"You were expected an hour and a half ago, Miss Dalton." Miss Barth's voice was reproving. It was as well to establish the lines of power from the first.

Keri chortled inwardly. Nice try, Miss Barth. "I would not leave without briefing my replacement, Miss Barth," she responded austerely. "The disruption to Mr. Simonds's routine will be severe as it is. I took what steps I deemed necessary to mitigate the impact as much as possible." Keri gave Miss Barth a straight look.

Miss Barth was taken aback. In spite of the bland exterior, Miss Dalton had teeth and seemed prepared to use them. She resolved to walk more warily. There had been indecent haste in obtaining the services of this woman, so obviously she had some necessary skill. Dain Randolph did not suffer fools at all, much less gladly. Miss Barth was no fool.

"I will tell Mr. Randolph you have arrived. You may

explain your delay directly to him." The look she gave Keri was smug. She flipped a switch, picked up the phone, and said in dulcet tones, "Miss Dalton has arrived, sir. Shall I send her in?"

The answer was obviously affirmative and she responded, "Yes, sir." She replaced the receiver and looked speculatively at Keri. "You may go in now, Miss Dalton."

Keri nodded coolly and opened the inner door.

CHAPTER 2

Keri stepped into the office and swept it with a lightning glance before her eyes jolted to a stop on the man standing behind the paper-laden desk. She didn't pause in her steady pace toward him, but inwardly she was reeling from a nasty shock! He was big, he was handsome, he was aggressively masculine, and she recognized all too well that appraising look in his eye. He was also the most attractive man she had ever set eyes upon and she felt an unexpected, and unwelcome, flutter in the pit of her stomach. She thinned her lips, gathered the cloak of her composure tightly about herself, and stopped on the opposite side of his desk. She eyed him warily from behind the shield of her glinting spectacles.

Dain himself was prey to a mixed bag of sensations, the strongest of which was sheer amazement. For *this* Schyler Van Metre was willing to break his engagement to Denise? Dain had no illusions whatsoever about his sister's nature. She was wild, beautiful, and passionate. She was also

33

spoiled, vindictive, and petulant when thwarted, but she was all woman. The woman who faced him now was an icicle, no, an iceberg. Chill efficiency radiated from her with tangible force. If a man touched her, he could draw back an ice-rimed hand.

Keri, in her turn, was assessing the man who faced her. He was the antithesis of Mr. Simonds in every way. Her heart sank. She doubted if he had even reached thirty yet. He was deeply tanned and his eyes, as green as her own, surveyed her coolly from across the desk. Dark brown hair lay sleekly against a well-shaped skull and just touched the collar of his striped beige shirt. He had shed his suit jacket, but his dark brown vest was buttoned, emphasizing the powerful spread of his shoulders and flat, narrow waist.

Schyler played hard. This man might play hard, but he worked hard as well. There was no softness anywhere about him. Each angle and plane of his handsome face was uncompromising and ruthless, and there was an arrogance and surety which boded ill for those who chose to cross him. A man to take what he wanted and a man who would be sure, very sure, of what he wanted.

Dain, in his turn, was making his own deeper, appraisal. There *had* to be something more to this woman than what was obvious to the immediate eye! He had met Schyler Van Metre and had sized him up easily. The man was a connoisseur and no thin-blooded, purse-mouthed spinster could hold Schyler's absorbed interest, and absorbed he was.

Schyler had told Denise frankly, and later Dain, that he had searched for her, finally given up in despair, and had succumbed to his father's pressures to wed after meeting Denise.

34

He had found Keri again through some unhoped for stroke of fortune, and this time she would not escape him. He now wished to be released from his engagement so that he might resume his relationship with Keri. Denise refused. She asked for time, pointing out how humiliating it would be if he jilted her within a mere two weeks from the time of their announced intention to marry. She also pointed out that she might be pregnant. Schyler could not deny the possibility. He had agreed to let the engagement stand for a reasonable length of time, for appearance's sake, but he stipulated that he would still be seeing Keri during that period of waiting, and as soon as the allotted time had passed, he would expect Denise to release him.

Denise had agreed reluctantly, but privately she vowed that Schyler was hers and Keri Dalton would pay for her effrontery. When Dain returned from London, he had been met by a distraught and blotchily tearful sister, who sobbed with calculated abandon on his broad chest.

The tale of Schyler's perfidy, her possible pregnancy, and the threat her fiancé's ex-mistress posed to her ultimate happiness poured forth in a disjointed, semi-hysterical stream of gasping sobs. Dain was disgusted, but she *was* his sister. He met with Schyler, who confirmed her story in the main, and who reiterated his determination to resume his relationship with Keri, but with a view to marriage this time. Dain's mouth had tightened to a grim line, but he had made no comment.

"Sit down, Miss Dalton," Dain gestured to a chair and watched as Keri arranged herself, purse on lap, hands tidily folded atop it. Her spine was ramrod stiff and her expression forbidding.

"You are late in arriving, Miss Dalton. I expect prompt

compliance with my orders. Have you any excuses?" His tone was cold.

"I briefed my replacement, sir." Keri's tone was anything but apologetic.

One of Dain's eyebrows shot up in disbelief. She was taking *him* to task! As had Miss Barth before him, he was discovering that the prim exterior hid an extremely efficient set of teeth, and that Keri's bite might well be much worse than her bark.

Keri was at the stage where she didn't care if he fired her on the spot. All of her instincts told her this man was more of a threat to her than Schyler had ever been. She hadn't liked his thorough appraisal of her face and figure as she stood before him and she feared those shrewd green eyes. Those eyes could all too easily see beneath the make-up-thin layer of her composure, and she wouldn't have to give him an inch before he would take a mile!

To her surprise he let that thrust pass without further comment. He sat at his desk and eyed her over his steepled fingers. "Mr. Simonds was unstinting in his praise of your abilities, Miss Dalton."

"Thank you, sir." Keri responded formally and briefly.

"I understand you speak several languages," he said, switching smoothly into French.

"I speak five, sir, in addition to English," she responded, also in French. If he wanted to play games, she would humor him.

"How were you able to acquire so many?" he questioned her.

Since he still spoke in French, she explained, continuing in the same language. "My father is in the army. I have traveled widely with my parents because the majority of his postings were abroad. A child absorbs languages easily when her playmates speak nothing but their own tongue. I speak French and German most fluently because I spent more of my formative years in countries where those languages were primary."

"And your parents? Where are they now?" he asked in fluent German.

"They are abroad on another assignment," she responded likewise.

He dropped back into English, evidently satisfied with her claims to knowledge of those two languages. "You came to us on personal recommendation from Charles Lawson and there seems to be no record of your educational or employment history. May I have a capsule version now?" The sentence was a question. The voice made it an order.

Keri sighed soundlessly. It could do no harm now, she supposed. Schyler knew where she was, so there was no longer any reason to hide her connection with Van Metre and Company. "Very well, sir." She gave in with no good grace. "I graduated from Georgetown University with a major in Political Science and minors in languages. I did six months' additional graduate work before deciding that I preferred to settle in the States for a while, rather than entering the State Department and being posted abroad. I was tired of traveling. I obtained a position as interim private secretary to Mr. Steven Hargood of Sunsur Oil Company for six months. I was then secretary to John DeLautre of Ardeen Manufacturing for a period of one year. I left that position and became secretary and assistant to Mr. Terrence Platt of Ectron Associates for a period of one year. I then became executive secretary to Mr. Carleton Van Metre of Van Metre and Company for a period of six months. I left that position six months ago for personal reasons. I have been employed by RanCo for the past three months in the position of secretary to Mr. Simonds." She finished her recitation in a level, emotionless voice and sat, hands still primly folded in her lap, awaiting further cross-examination.

"A rather brief and varied history for one so capable, Miss Dalton," he said musingly.

Keri waited apprehensively for more probing questions. Simple arithmetic would tell him that her age was at sharp variance with her appearance, but he seemed to lose interest in the game. He rose and said dismissively, "Miss Barth will show you to your office. She will brief you on your current duties."

Keri rose with the alacrity of relief. She wondered how Charles would feel about getting her another job? Not whoopingly enthusiastic, she imagined. Mr. Simondses didn't grow on trees. She'd just have to trust to her skill at makeup and a frosty manner.

She learned several things during her first two days working for Dain Randolph. One, that he did indeed do enough work to keep his three secretaries comfortably busy, and two, that he made her very nervous.

She was not called to his office at any time during those first days, but several times she looked up from her work to find him staring at her from the doorway of the office she shared with Mrs. Covey. She had the fleeting impression of a cat poised before the mousehole, ready to sweep up the unwary morsel with his sharp claws at his leisure. He never spoke, but he wouldn't move away immediately either. It was almost as though he conducted a war of nerves, which was a ridiculous notion, she told herself crossly.

Miss Barth had noted Dain's inexplicable interest in the

38

new secretary and gnashed her pearly teeth. She was subtly snide to Keri and received chilling politeness for her pains. Keri had no desire whatsoever to supplant Miss Barth in whatever claim to affection she had on Mr. Randolph, and the sooner Miss Barth realized that fact, the happier they'd all be.

Keri drove her Porsche out of the company parking lot each evening with the sensation of a prisoner escaping vile durance by the slightest of margins. She never saw Dain Randolph observing her incongruous vehicle with speculative eyes. He had come to the conclusion that Miss Dalton was indeed an iceberg, with nine-tenths of her personality concealed beneath that ice-cold shell.

Schyler called her Wednesday night, right after she got in from work, to ask if he might come over for a short time. She refused to see him, and to her surprise, he accepted her rejection in good spirits. Twenty minutes later he appeared at her door with a steaming hot pizza, a bottle of Mateus rosé, and an engaging grin. As before, he took the precaution of putting his foot in the door the moment she opened it.

"I hope you haven't started dinner yet, Keri, my love," he said blithely, balancing the pizza carton with careful fingers.

"Beware of the Dutch bearing gifts," Keri misquoted dryly, and prepared to close the door, foot notwithstanding. Just before Schyler's neatly shod toes were caught between immovable object and irresistible force (door jamb and door), the telephone startled them both with its imperative summons. Keri hesitated and was lost.

Schyler took advantage of her momentary inattention to consolidate his position inside the door and she looked at him with frustrated irritation. "You'd better answer your phone, Keri darling," he advised. "It sounds impatient. I'll put the pizza in the kitchen and set the table."

"You stay out of my kitchen, Schyler," she said heatedly as she picked up the phone. "Hello?" she snapped ungraciously into the receiver.

"Am I interrupting something important, Miss Dalton?" came the bland voice through the receiver.

"I beg your pardon? Who is this?" Keri was suddenly fed to the teeth with all men. She glared at Schyler who, in spite of her adjurations, was going into the kitchen. She'd never get him out of her apartment, thanks to this inopportune idiot on the phone.

"This is Dain Randolph, Miss Dalton," came the unabashed reply. "I won't keep you since you seem to be entertaining, but I wanted to tell you not to come into the office tomorrow morning."

The last straw, Keri fulminated. Riddles yet! But before she had time to comment that that suited her just fine, the bland voice continued.

"I have an important conference tomorrow morning at nine A.M. I am taking you with me to take notes because several of the gentlemen involved speak no English. Please be ready outside your apartment building promptly at eight fifteen." When Keri didn't reply at once, he said sharply, "Is that clear, Miss Dalton?"

"Yes, sir, very clear. I'll be ready, sir," she acquiesced tonelessly.

There was a long pause and then he said, "Enjoy your evening, Miss Dalton," and hung up. Keri glared at the receiver and then glared at Schyler, who stood in the kitchen doorway, smiling smugly.

"The table's set, the wine poured, and the pizza is your favorite kind. Who was that?"

"My boss," she answered automatically. "He's taking me to a conference in the morning so I'm not to go into the office tomorrow. He called to tell me about it." She gave in to the inevitable. "Schyler, if I eat the pizza with you, will you promise that you'll leave after that, without any trouble?"

Schyler knew when he'd pushed a victory as far as it would go. He raised his hand as though taking an oath. "I promise. I am on my best behavior." He seated Keri at the small dinette table with practiced flair and proceeded to make himself agreeable. He fully understood that Keri didn't trust him as far as she could see him, and he had to admit she had plenty of cause. God help him if she ever found out just how much cause, but she was an obsession with him now and he had to have her. He wouldn't allow himself to contemplate failure.

To Keri's surprise, Schyler, for once, was as good as his word. He put himself to the task of entertaining her during the meal and she had to admit, to herself only, that it was a superlative example of how to charm a wary bird, with herself as the wariest bird ever hatched! When the meal was finished, he helped her clear away the dishes, accepted her refusal to allow him to dry while she washed them and went biddably away.

It was like being braced against a shove which never came. She felt off balance and extremely suspicious. Schyler was trying a new tack, that much was clear. It was up to her to show him that this tack wasn't going to work any better than the others had. She'd also have to talk to the landlord about getting a peephole installed in the door. No more opening the door without knowing who was on the other side!

The next morning Keri rose early. She stood for a long

time, contemplating her wardrobe. After much deliberation she chose a trimly tailored olive green suit which had the interesting effect of making her look as though she might be in the first stages of jaundice. It also broadened her hips and shoulders just enough to destroy the clean lines of her normal figure. The whole effect, when she had completed her makeup and hairdo, was exquisitely subtle. There was not one thing glaringly amiss, but the totality left her colorless and drab. She placed her glasses firmly on her nose and smiled primly at herself in the mirror. Staid, efficient, and depressingly dull . . . exactly what she had striven to achieve.

In a defiant freakish fit of humor, she dabbed on her favorite perfume, Charmé, a fragrance so at variance with her current appearance that it signified for her a final, mocking thumb of the nose. She gathered her purse, stenographic notebook, and a supply of freshly sharpened pencils and locked the door of her apartment behind her.

There was no one in the elevator going down, for which she was grateful. She had no desire to have to explain her appearance to someone who knew her well in her normal mode of dress. When put into words, the whole idea had a tendency to sound both conceited and a trifle paranoid.

Promptly at 8:15 Dain and the car arrived at the front door of her apartment building. The uniformed chauffeur hastened around to open the back door and Keri was ceremoniously assisted inside. When she had settled herself comfortably, Dain quietly told the chauffeur to drive on, then pressed the button which closed the sliding glass partition between the driver's compartment and the back seat. He turned his attention to Keri.

"Good morning, Miss Dalton," he said conventionally.

"I'm glad to see that punctuality *is* one of your virtues after all."

Keri's lips compressed slightly but she merely replied, "Good morning, Mr. Randolph," sternly repressing the impulse to snap back at him. A colorless secretary did not make cutting remarks to her employer.

She could feel him watching her, waiting for her to rise to his provocation, but she contemplated the passing scenery with perfect equanimity. It was a mere pinprick, after all, easily ignored. She felt unwontedly triumphant.

Dain studied the clean line of her profile. In the shaded light of the car the sallowness of her complexion lost its force and he could concentrate on the bone structure without the distraction of color tones. The chin was sweetly curved, if a trifle obstinate, and the nose, where it was not weighted down by those unattractive spectacles, was classically modeled. The lips were fuller than they looked full face, especially the lower one, and Dain wondered how she had achieved that thinning effect. It must have to do with the color of the lipstick she used, he finally decided.

Looking at her from the side, the shielding effect of the heavy glasses was diminished and he became aware of the dark length of her eyelashes and the high cheekbones. With a sudden shock he realized that, in profile, she was beautiful. He sucked in air sharply and she turned to look at him curiously.

Sitting so close to her he realized several other things as well. At such close range he could study her eyes through her glasses and he saw that they were a dark sea-deep green, much the color of his own. He also realized that her lenses had no magnifying or distorting effect, which meant that they were either pitifully weak or mere glass with no prescriptive strength at all. In other words, they were part and parcel of a disguise. She was deliberately, for some unfathomable reason, making herself look like a frump!

He shut his eyes, the better to concentrate on these revelations, and at once became aware of the perfume she wore. It had subtly teased his senses since she had entered the car, but the distraction of her outward appearance had pushed its message into his subconscious. Now it was surfacing and he could match it to the inner vision of that flawless profile.

Green eyes, titian hair, and a neck like a swan's. He'd take a bet with any odds that the body underneath that chaste and chastening suit was just as lovely as the rest of her, and just as deceptively packaged. No wonder Schyler Van Metre was panting on the trail. A cruel smile curved his mouth.

"This is an extremely important conference today, Miss Dalton. Accuracy in your notes is essential." Dain's eyes opened to survey the impassive face of the woman who watched him warily and for a long moment their eyes locked in a silent struggle. Although her face remained inexpressive, behind her glasses the dark green eyes carried a message hard to define except that it wasn't friendly.

Keri turned her profile to Dain again, breaking the eye contact. "Of course, Mr. Randolph. I always strive for complete accuracy. I am sure you will find the quality of my notes most satisfactory, sir." Keri kept her voice colorless with an effort and continued, "Do you wish to brief me on the purpose of the meeting or give me any special instructions before we arrive, sir?" He nodded, but waited for her to finish all her questions. She continued, "Would you prefer the final form in the original languages or would you prefer a completely translated copy?"

He looked at her narrowly. "Will you take the notes in the languages of origin?" he asked curiously.

"Of course, sir, if that is what you desire." Keri maintained her impassive mien. She looked at him guilelessly for a short moment before facing forward again.

Dain's mouth compressed. Subtly, in a way he couldn't voice a precise objection to, she was getting to him. She was a caricature of the superefficient secretary and he didn't doubt she could do all she promised. Her notes would be impeccable and he would stake RanCo that she wouldn't miss an important word or sign during the whole conference. And if she *sir*red him one more time he would strangle her!

In keeping with her deliberately drab appearance, Keri seemed determined to project an image of machinelike efficiency which obscured her reality as anything more than a piece of office furniture. If he hadn't already been curious about her, it might have worked, for a time, at least. But, as with all defenses which depend on the concealment by camouflage, once alerted to the presence of the prey a predator can easily strip away the ephemeral shield to expose the quivering, tender morsel beneath.

He would strip away her pathetic, evasive ploys at his leisure, he decided. It shouldn't be difficult at all to prize her out of her shell of respectable drabness, even if he had to crack it a bit in the process.

He began to brief her on the topics of the conference and the men who would be present. Keri pulled out her notebook and began to take notes, her pencil slipping rapidly over the page. He gave her a list of the names of those to be present plus a thumbnail sketch of each. He watched as she listed each man and appended a symbol beside each name, different in each case. When he asked her the sig nificance of the symbols she explained. "They tell me who said what . . . a sort of shorthand shorthand." There was just the faintest hint of a smile playing around her mouth, so elusive he couldn't truly be sure it was really there.

When the conference started, Keri blended into the background with the ease of a chameleon. Dain eyed her sourly, half admiring, half irritated at her consummate ability to efface herself. None of the other men at the conference seemed even aware of her presence, save as the sibilant slide of pencil over paper or the hand which passed coffee cups when breaks were taken to moisten throats dry from wrangling.

Keri was an irritating burr in Dain's consciousness, unobtrusive but stabbing sharply at unexpected times. From the corner of his eye he discovered that he was distracted by the smooth length of shapely leg which was visible to him, free from the enigma of her face.

If he swiveled his head a bit further, her hands came into his line of vision, tracing symbols with deft rapidity over the notebook. Graceful, long-fingered, with short, oval nails buffed to a healthy sheen but innocent of polish. She wore no rings, only a businesslike chain-linked watch to point to the delicacy of her wrists, and Dain wondered suddenly how a glowing emerald would look on those slender fingers. With irritated discipline he dismissed the fanciful thoughts and wrenched his attention back to the conference.

Keri was well-satisfied with the course of the role she played. No man paid more than the most cursory of attention to her and if her lips curved into a self-congratulatory smile while she bent her head over her racing pencil, no one saw it, not even Dain. Her skills were extended but not overtaxed and she enjoyed the sensation, for she always welcomed a challenge, especially one she had no real difficulty in meeting.

When the conference broke for a meal, Keri hung back, planning to find her own lunch and enjoy the break from the ceaseless recording. The men agreed to make do with a mere forty-five minutes of conviviality, but she was in no position to quibble. She'd take what she could get.

The firm clasp around her elbow was unexpected and unwelcome. She looked down at the hand that held her so firmly and back up into the ironic green eyes, keeping what she hoped was a bland expression to match the one on the hard, handsome face that closely scrutinized her own.

"Going somewhere, Miss Dalton?" asked the smooth, deep voice.

"Yes, sir, to my lunch," she answered with surprise, which she hoped wasn't overdone.

"Your lunch is this way, Miss Dalton, with me." As he was speaking, Dain was irresistibly propelling Keri along beside him, in the opposite direction from the one the other men were taking.

Keri knew better than to argue. Docile, efficient secretaries never gainsay the boss, but her mouth was tight and her nostrils slightly pinched as she walked beside him to a single elevator, which he activated with a key. To her dismay, they rose instead of descending. Dain maintained his clasp on her elbow, slightly eased in strength, even while they were alone in the cubicle. Keri prayed earnestly that they wouldn't get trapped between floors through some freak celestial joke perpetrated by a malicious prankster of a god. She already knew, the farther away she could stay from Dain Randolph, the safer she'd be! There was danger in every one of his seventy-four inches of long bone and hard muscle.

When the elevator slid smoothly to a stop, there was an agonizing pause before the doors opened to release them. Keri hoped that Dain hadn't noticed that she had been holding her breath and she tried not to let it all out in too audible a whoosh of relief. The commanding hand relentlessly urged her out of the elevator and they walked forward into a luxurious apartment.

Through a floor-to-ceiling glass wall she could see a table laid for two on a small terrace. A silent-footed servant came forward, rather in the manner of a genie out of a bottle, and murmured greetings respectfully to Dain. He acknowledged the greeting and ordered the man to serve the salad while they washed their hands, reminding him that they were going to be pressed for time.

Dain directed Keri toward a luxuriously appointed bathroom, choosing to utilize the one attached to the master suite himself. She washed and dried her hands in a state of bemusement and no little trepidation. This was going to be tougher than she thought, with Dain in such close proximity for so long a time. Those deep green eyes were windows to an uncomfortably keen brain, one which could strip pretense away as easily as an ecdysiast peels away her gaudy garb with a flirtatious flip of a hip.

She went back out into the living room, head high and chin tilted at a determined angle. He was waiting for her. He escorted her solicitously, giving her the feeling that she was a favored and slightly doddering maiden aunt, onto the sunlit terrace. He pulled out her chair, seated her, and took his place across from her. Keri immediately became defensively absorbed in the deliciously crisp green salad. He allowed her three peaceful bites before he pounced.

"Take your glasses off, Miss Dalton." The order was flat and expected obedience.

Keri's startled eyes flashed to the hard face that watched her so intently, her own face unguarded momentarily and as shocked as if he'd ordered her to strip naked. Then her own defenses reasserted themselves and she surveyed him coolly.

"Why?" She questioned both his motives and his authority bluntly.

His face darkened. He wasn't used to being questioned. He lifted his hand swiftly, and before Keri had a chance to jerk her head away, he pulled the glasses off her nose. He held them up and looked through the lenses, his mouth curling in a smile that held little amusement. He tossed them contemptuously onto the table between them, and they slid to a stop against the salt shaker. Keri's hand twitched as though to grab them, but with an effort of will she refrained from doing so. She looked at Dain with a perfectly composed face, lips thinned and prim.

"Stop looking like an outraged old-maid schoolteacher, Miss Dalton," Dain advised her with asperity. "Those spectacles you've been covering behind are nothing but pure glass. You don't need them at all."

"No, I don't," Keri admitted serenely. "I have perfect vision." Now she took another bite of her salad, chewed it reflectively, swallowed, and began to eat steadily with outward composure.

"You're certainly a cool one," Dain said with unwilling admiration.

Keri could have told him that inwardly she was quaking like an aspen leaf in a high wind, but she managed to continue eating steadily. Each bite scraped down a throat that threatened to close tightly from tension, but no sign of her inward agitation appeared on her smooth face.

Dain let it rest as they were served with the main course, but as soon as the servant had departed to the kitchen regions, he returned to the attack. "Why the charade, Miss Dalton? You could be an attractive woman, but you choose to masquerade as a fusty old maid."

With a sigh of resignation Keri finished the bit of quiche she had been eating and put down her fork. "I prefer to keep my business and private lives separate, Mr. Randolph. I found that impossible when I appear at work in my normal guise." She continued with a defensive tone. "I am sorry if that sounds conceited or vain, but believe me, it is merely the statement of a painfully learned fact." She picked up her fork and resumed her meal.

"That's why the varied employment history?" he questioned perceptively.

"That's why."

Dain made no direct comment for a long moment, seeming to reflect on her words, and then he attacked directly. "I am giving a reception for the gentlemen of the conference tomorrow night. You will be there to act as my hostess and you will, by then, have shed this pose and be dressed in your normal style."

"And if I refuse?" Keri's green eyes glittered furiously.

Dain's face took on frighteningly ruthless lines and he spoke with menacing softness, "You will not refuse, Miss Dalton. You will carry out the duties required of you as one of my confidential secretaries, as I direct you."

Keri was defeated and they both knew it. The choice was most clearly laid out before her. If she wished to keep her job, she would do so on Dain Randolph's terms, no other way. Somehow he knew her for what she was, and once he had pierced her masquerade, it was useless to her.

"Very well, sir," she admitted herself bested. "Shall I handle the arrangements for the reception?"

"No, Miss Barth has them well in hand. She will brief you on them tomorrow morning." He smiled slightly to himself. "She has also been informed that you are to act as hostess because of your linguistic abilities."

Keri's lips twitched irrepressibly and for a brief instant a current of humor ran between them. Miss Barth was not going to be pleased by Keri's transformation from ugly duckling to svelte swan and they both knew it. Keri's amusement was short-lived, however, for she knew all too well what problems coping with a jealous co-worker could present, and she was sadly familiar with the Miss Barths of the world. She had no desire to engage in a struggle for power, but Miss Barth was going to see it as a direct threat when Keri unexpectedly and dramatically blossomed into a tiger lily. Keri sighed wistfully. Life had been so pleasant for the three months as Mr. Simonds's secretary. Now those months resembled the eye of a hurricane, and the winds of conflict and destructive force were rising once again around her. Schyler had been a tempest in a teapot. Dain Randolph was like a devastating typhoon.

She refused dessert, picked up her glasses, and replaced them firmly upon her nose. Dain scowled horribly, but Keri looked right back at him with calm determination. Tomorrow night would be soon enough for her transformation and she had no intention of going back to that conference room different from how she had left it, especially after a luncheon à deux with her boss. Prim she came in, prim she would go back out!

"Is this your apartment?" she questioned him, looking

for a subject to fill the time while he ate the fruit he had chosen as a finish to his meal. She didn't for a minute think it was, because the whole apartment had the slightly sterile air of a first-class hotel, but she had no desire to sit in intimate silence with him. So she made aimless conversation. She wasn't exactly *nervous,* but she was a long way from being at ease in his presence.

From the sardonic gleam in his eyes she knew he was fully aware of her disquiet, but he played the game by his own particular rules and answered her civilly enough. "In a manner of speaking, it is. This building belongs to RanCo and we keep this apartment for the convenience of visiting dignitaries and for the times when entertaining on a smaller scale is desirable."

There was not the slightest hint of an innuendo in his tone, but Keri knew he was laughing silently. He was totally at ease as he lounged in his chair, finishing his succulent peach. *Well, why shouldn't he be,* she thought crossly. *He's certainly had everything his way, and I'm feeling a perfect fool.*

Somehow she endured the rest of the tête-à-tête and the afternoon that followed. By firmly cramming the speculations and what-do-I-do-nows down below the level of conscious worry, she managed to maintain her morning level of efficiency, but the effort left her feeling drained and limp by the time the conference concluded.

Fortunately Dain was engrossed in paper work during the drive back to her apartment and she was left in peace, ostensibly to review and plan the transcription of her notes. She began to extract a precis of the salient points of discussion plus position statements for each of the participants in the conference. Dain had not requested it, but it was standard practice as far as Keri was concerned.

She was determined she'd also have the verbatim transcription ready to lay on his desk first thing tomorrow. She knew he expected her to spend the morning on the transcription, but it was a point of honor to have it ready at his hand when he sat down, even if it meant she was up half the night. She'd show him she was an executive secretary, not just a pretty face!

Keri took a composed departure from Dain in front of her building, smiling warmly at the chauffeur as he helped her from the car, and causing him to take another look at the plain Miss Dalton. That smile really had something! Dain caught the fringe of the smile as it rayed over the chauffeur and his mouth quirked in sardonic amusement. No smiles for me, eh, girl? Well, we'll see about that, won't we?

CHAPTER 3

It didn't take half the night to complete the transcription, but Keri was glad to rip the last sheet of paper out of her portable electric typewriter. She stacked the sheaf of papers neatly and debated whether to pour herself a final cup of coffee. A glance at the clock decided her, and she emptied the rest of the liquid in the percolator down the sink drain. She had a feeling that she was going to need a good night's sleep!

She'd made a sketchy meal when she got home, but had been too eager to get started on the evening's work to do more than open a few cans and improvise with dabs of leftovers. Now, with the impetus gone, her stomach announced its presence with a gentle reminder. Placating it with a bologna and cheese sandwich, she finished proof-reading her evening's output, and well satisfied, went to bed to sleep the undisturbed sleep of the just.

The next morning, moved by a perhaps foolhardy desire to impress upon Dain Randolph that he couldn't dictate totally to her, and the equal desire to avoid conflict for as long as possible with the possessive Miss Barth, Keri decided to delay her emergence from chrysalis until the evening reception. She chose a mud-brown tailored suit, teamed it with just the wrong shade of yellow blouse, and scraped her hair back into a bun for the last time.

Defiantly she splashed on Charmé, jammed her glasses on her nose, and almost sneered at her mirror. "Nos morituri te salutamus," she said aloud to her unresponsive image and left the apartment.

She was deliberately early and slipped into Dain's office well before he was due to arrive. She laid the completed pile of transcriptions, plus her other additions, squarely in the middle of his desk. Since neither Miss Barth nor Mrs. Covey had made an appearance, Keri decided to fortify herself with a cup of the surprisingly excellent coffee dispensed by the small canteen on the executive floor.

She was leaning casually against the counter, chatting to the young girl who ran the canteen, when the widening eyes and faltering words of her companion alerted her. Her head swiveled slowly, looking over her left shoulder. Dain Randolph loomed behind her and with a slightly sinking heart Keri straightened.

"Good morning, Mr. Randolph," she said politely and waited.

"Come to my office, Miss Dalton," he ordered peremptorily and strode off down the corridor.

Keri stood looking after him for a moment, wondering if her spurt of defiance was going to be such a good idea after all. His obvious fury was quelling. The young girl gave her a sympathetic smile as she accepted Keri's cup, but to Keri it held strong elements of pity, and she could feel the girl's gaze following her progress down the corridor. More juice for the grapevine, she thought wryly.

Before she went into Dain's office, she dashed into her own and snatched up a dictation pad and a pencil. With them and what she devoutly hoped was an impervious, deadpan expression, she opened the door and went in. He was standing behind his desk, still wearing the same forbidding expression with which he had surveyed her at the canteen.

He went right to the attack. "I expect obedience from my secretaries, *Miss* Dalton," he rasped.

She didn't pretend to misunderstand him. "I shall be suitably dressed for the reception this evening, Mr. Randolph," she assured him stiffly, not giving an inch.

Something black and dangerous flared deep in the back of his eyes and she covertly watched a small muscle jump along the hard bone of his jaw line. She met his eyes steadily, but only she knew the effort it cost her. Suddenly she knew that this man could be utterly ruthless. The Van Metres might have been descended from a pirate, but this man would be his modern-day counterpart. There was a natural air of command and inflexibility of purpose emanating from him in an aura so tangible she could almost see rather than sense it.

He had meant, had expected, to see her dressed normally at the office this morning and her failure to do so had, for some reason, disproportionately angered him. She wouldn't have thought him an unreasoning autocrat, but unless she were to think that her failure to appear in her normal guise had disappointed him, that he was eager to see what she *really* looked like, she could only conclude that he expected every order to be immediately carried out.

57

With the inspiration born of desperation she gestured at the papers she had left on his desk earlier. His eyes dropped to follow her motion, but before she could say something, a most welcome interruption occurred. Miss Barth, glancing through the doorway, noticed that Keri was in seemingly intimate conversation with Mr. Randolph and some instinctive, territorial reaction brought her bustling in with the morning mail.

Keri relaxed in relief. Dain glared at the unfortunate Miss Barth, who stuttered in dismayed explanation. "I . . . I thought you'd like your morning mail, Mr. Randolph. M-may I bring you a cup of coffee?"

Seizing the chance with both hands, Keri murmured, "I'll get to my own work, Mr. Randolph," and exited with graceful haste.

The rest of the day was strained. A resentful Miss Barth gave Keri a briefing on the reception arrangements and Keri caught the other woman studying her closely several times with a suspicious intensity. Keri did nothing but look blandly back at her every time their eyes met, but she knew, with a sinking heart, that when she came to work on Monday, Miss Barth was not going to be pleased. She might already have suspicions, but the reality of Keri's natural appearance was not going to come as a pleasant surprise to her co-worker. Keri was refusing to think just what it was going to be to Mr. Dain Randolph.

Mrs. Covey seemed oblivious to the cross- and undercurrents that swirled within the office suite. She typed and filed with all of her usual phlegm, but she accepted Keri's overture for lunch with flattering alacrity; Keri didn't deceive herself that it was solely for the pleasure of her company. Mrs. Covey might not be in competition for Mr. Randolph's attentions, but she had all the normal curiosi

ties of her sex and she had tried more than once to genteelly pump Keri. Keri had equally genteelly remained un-
pumpable.

Unfortunately, the old order changeth and Keri wasn't
going to be able to remain aloof if she planned to continue
working at RanCo much longer. She was going to have to
tap the office grapevine for information and Mrs. Covey
was sure to prove a convenient as well as fruitful source.

They chose a small nearby restaurant because Keri felt
the need to escape totally from the environs of RanCo for
even so short a time as the lunch break. Miss Barth had
smugly informed her fellow secretaries that she and Mr.
Randolph would be sharing a working lunch. Keri silently
wished her the best of luck with what the other secretary
obviously saw as a heaven-sent opportunity.

While Keri was pouring oil and vinegar over her chef's
salad, and wondering how to find out what she wanted to
know with as much subtlety as was possible in the circumstances, Mrs. Covey obligingly saved her the trouble. She
flew to the subject of Dain Randolph like a homing pigeon
to its favorite roost.

"Isn't Mr. Randolph an interesting man?" she enthused.

"Mmm, yes, he is," Keri agreed warily, and speared a
lettuce leaf.

Agreement seemed to be the only spur Mrs. Covey
needed because the river of her confidences reached flood
proportions immediately. Keri was rapidly brought up-to-
date on the fact that Mrs. Covey had worked for Dain's
father until sudden ill health had forced his involuntary
surrender of the reins to Dain when that young man was
barely out of college, where evidently few academic and
social honors had escaped him.

In fact, according to Mrs. Covey, little escaped Dain if he chose, be it women or business coups. Though yet short of thirty, he had put together a number of outstandingly complicated takeovers, divestations, and mergers, all of them shockingly profitable to RanCo. He had recently been in Europe on just such another major enterprise, and the staff and stockholders of RanCo confidently expected the latest to be no different from the previous in terms of success and profitability.

Keri didn't doubt it in the least. Latter-day pirate or modern version thereof, he'd be successful no matter what his occupation. He wore the arrogant, unmistakable look of power like a cloak—an inborn, integral part of a powerful personality.

Then Mrs. Covey switched from the public to the private life of Keri's daunting employer. In exhaustive detail she told Keri far more than she wanted to know about Dain Randolph the man, confirming with every word what Keri had feared since she had confronted him across the width of his desk that first day.

Like a rake in Regency days, Dain had adroitly evaded the marriage mart, choosing instead to play, when he played, among the sophisticated and worldly, most of whom played the game superbly and often. Mrs. Covey was acidic about Miss Barth's so obvious aspirations, assuring Keri that Mr. Randolph never looked among his employees for his, as she delicately termed it, liaisons.

Keri wasn't sure if Mrs. Covey meant this statement for warning or reassurance. She would like to be able to accept it as reassurance, but the hard, appraising eyes which had stripped away her camouflage so easily were anything but impersonal. She didn't know *why* he was so interested, but the fact remained that he *was!* Something had triggered his attention and now Dain Randolph was exhibiting more than common interest in an employee.

"Has Mr. Randolph any other family?" Keri questioned idly, when Mrs. Covey paused for breath.

"Hmph, yes. A sister six years younger," responded Mrs. Covey in portentous tones. "And a right bitch that one is. Mr. Randolph and his father have pulled her out of more scrapes than *I* care to think of. They've spoiled her rotten because her mother died when she was just a little girl and she's used to having the world laid out on a carpet for her. I hear she's recently gotten herself engaged, so now there'll be three men to indulge her. She hasn't been around much because Mr. Randolph's been away, but you can be sure we'll be seeing more of her, sweeping in, nodding graciously to the serfs, and snarling like a sand cat whenever things don't go her way. She's got claws, that one, and isn't choosy about whom she uses them on, except for Mr. Randolph, of course. She's honey sweet and purring with *him!*"

And without losing a beat, Mrs. Covey looked shrewdly at Keri and said, "And what about you, my dear? When are you going to quit hiding behind those dowdy clothes and prim manner?"

It was too sudden a move for Keri to mask her reaction. Her mouth fell open with shock while Mrs. Covey chuckled quietly, well satisfied with her broadside. Keri looked at the dumpy little woman sitting opposite her and began to smile in her own turn. She laughed softly and ruefully.

"I've worked at RanCo three months with nary a raised eyebrow and now, in the space of two days, two people have seen through me. There must be clearer vision in the rarefied air of the executive suite," she finished dryly.

"Mr. Randolph being the other one with clear vision," Mrs. Covey stated without any fear of contradiction.

"Yes," Keri sighed. "I'm under orders to cease and desist, starting tonight at the reception." She grinned with just the slightest touch of mischief. "I was supposed to start this morning, but decided tonight would be a more appropriate time."

"Monday should be most interesting," averred Mrs. Covey, grimacing. "Elise Barth is in for an unpalatable shock. She's been Miss Glamor of the office for the past three years, for all the good it's done her, but she won't relish being supplanted."

"Are you so sure I'll . . . er . . . supplant her?" Keri asked curiously. "She's very attractive."

"Hmm, yes, attractive," Mrs. Covey agreed. "She makes the most of what she's got, I admit, but I expect that you don't even have to make anything of what you've got to bug out a few eyes. Why'd you do it, child?"

"Protective camouflage," Keri said shortly. "I got tired of wearing out my tennis shoes being chased around the desk. I had the idea that it would be nice to keep my business and private lives separate and it worked like a charm for three whole months. Blast!" Keri pounded her fist softly on the table top in frustration.

She took off her glasses and rubbed the bridge of her nose absently, but didn't notice the widening of Mrs. Covey's eyes when she saw Keri without them for the first time. Keri had eaten off her lipstick and the natural rich coloration of her lips emphasized the lovely shape of her mouth. With the glasses removed, Mrs. Covey could, for the moment, understand Keri's high wear-out rate of tennis shoes. Elise Barth was definitely not going to be pleased!

The two women finished lunch in silence, gloomy on Keri's part, thoughtful on Mrs. Covey's. The older woman hid a shrewd brain and a dry sense of humor beneath her unprepossessing exterior. She liked Keri and wished her well, but not even the most optimistic of Pollyannas could foresee anything but storms ahead for the young woman. Elise Barth would make her life miserable if she could, out of spite and jealousy, and even though Dain Randolph had never dallied with a RanCo employee to Mrs. Covey's knowledge (and it was comprehensive . . . she was *very* astute), she had a feeling that he just might make an exception in Keri's case.

He had so far displayed an unprecedented interest in obtaining her services as secretary, and Mrs. Covey didn't for one minute believe that it was because of Keri's facility in languages. And now, by Keri's own admission, he was going so far as to dictate to her about her appearance. Very interesting indeed!

Keri's afternoon was mercifully shortened because Dain brusquely ordered her to leave early so that she would have plenty of time to prepare for the evening ahead. The look he gave her as he issued this pronouncement was explicit. Keri and Dain both missed the hastily hidden smile on Mrs. Covey's face as she sat at her desk, an interested spectator to this charged confrontation between employer and employee. She smothered a chuckle at the glare of pure dislike that Keri shot at Dain's back as he left the office, but her "Knock 'em dead, Keri honey" was full of fellow feeling and Keri threw her a grateful smile as she left for the day.

Keri seriously considered Mrs. Covey's injunction as she drove home through the relatively uncrowded streets. She could, if she chose, knock 'em dead as Mrs. Covey said. She had a dress guaranteed to give every man within fifty feet of her galloping high blood pressure and she was very tempted to pull it out, but saner, second thoughts prevailed.

The last thing in the world she wanted to do was give Dain Randolph the "come hither" and the dress would be construed as nothing short of an open invitation to seduction by such a man. She'd better opt for cool elegance, and she had a dress for that occasion too. It was a severely plain Thai silk of a green-bronze that managed to enhance the depth of her eyes and the richness of her hair. The classic simplicity of its cut plus the figure beneath it did the rest, although the slit up the right leg which offered glimpses of an elegant stocking-sheathed leg to just above the knee as she walked, reminded the onlooker that she was a woman, mysterious and just that little bit provocative.

She lazed for a relaxing half hour in a high drift of scented bubbles, washed her hair, and set it. She ate a fairly substantial supper because, while there would be a more than adequate buffet table, it would be her job to circulate, not to nibble.

She considered the evening before her with extremely mixed feelings. Her sense of the ridiculous was stimulated by the stir she was going to cause among the men whom she had met at the conference. They just weren't going to be able to believe she was the same self-effacing secretary who had sat so primly in their midst. On the other hand, her sudden emergence into the limelight was going to make her the prey of some rather nasty speculations and, in all probability, to some unpleasant (to Keri) suggestions from some of the "gentlemen" of the conference. She made a bet with herself as to which ones were the most likely.

Well, those she could handle. It wouldn't be the first time! It was the longer term problem of Dain Randolph that she wasn't sure she could handle. The combination of experienced sensual challenge and potently attractive masculinity that he projected was devastatingly dangerous. Oh, well, forewarned (thanks to Mrs. Covey and her own common sense) is forearmed, she hoped.

When she was dressed and ready to leave, the mirror that had reflected the prim secretary in the morning showed her a far different image. Her hair shone in burnished glory as long curls cascaded from a Psyche knot. Her only jewelry, except for her skillfully highlighted green eyes that glowed like emeralds in a frame of dark bronze lashes, were gold filigree flower earrings set into the lobes of her small flat ears and a matching ring on her right forefinger. Dark amber topazes were set into the hearts of the flowers.

The mandarin collar of her dress caressed the base of the slender neck that supported her head so proudly and the tantalizing V-neck was frogged shut just above the lush swell of her breasts. Demure, but promising hidden richness. No longer did her lipstick hide the contours of her mouth, and her skin, freed from the disguising powder, had regained its warm apricot bloom, soft and smooth.

The transformation was complete and incredible, and to the man who stood with hand raised to knock, just as she opened the door, breathtaking. Keri paused in surprise, unconsciously framed in the doorway, confronting this unexpected, and unwelcome, apparition. His hand dropped forgotten to his side and his eyes shone with an odd glitter.

"My God, now I understand," he muttered, shaken. "What man wouldn't?"

"I beg your pardon?" Keri inquired frostily.

"I was making mental apology to someone," was the obscure explanation.

The appearance of her boss, clad in the severe black and white of evening dress, on her threshold was not calculated to calm Keri, and his cryptic words seemed all of a piece with his incomprehensible behavior. She was, however, afraid she knew what his next words were going to be, and she was right.

"I'll take you to the reception," he informed her, prepared to override and totally ignore her expected protest.

"But I . . ." Keri began to expostulate when the phone cut demandingly across her words.

It was a bad replay of the time Schyler had appeared at her door, she thought with exasperation as she watched Dain consolidate his position inside, much as Schyler had several nights before. She wasn't surprised either to discover that this time it was Schyler on the other end of the phone. Who else? She sighed in deepest exasperation.

"Hello, Schyler . . . No, Schyler, you cannot come over . . . . Because I won't *be* here starting about sixty seconds from now!" She banged down the phone sharply.

"Lover's tiff?" Dain drawled.

"No!" Keri snapped, up to her ears with men in general and Schyler in particular, and certainly in no mood for complicated explanations to a man whose business it wasn't anyway. In more moderate tones she continued. "I don't suppose it will do me any good to say that I'd prefer to take my own car?"

66

He shook his head just once and she picked up her purse from where she had laid it down to answer the phone, prepared to precede him from the apartment with no good grace. He tested the door to be sure it had locked firmly behind them, followed her to the elevator, and leaned around her to punch the summoning button. Without moving an inch, she seemed to compress slightly to avoid the slightest physical contact with him. His mouth took on an ominous tightness and when the elevator door opened at their floor, he grasped her elbow firmly to usher her inside.

She stood stiffly and quietly by his side during the short descent, too wise to make an issue by pulling away from him, but sharply conscious of the hard strength of his fingers and the warmth of his palm as it lay against the inside of her elbow. Even through the fabric of her sleeve the heat of his body reached out to hers and she was starkly aware again of his personal, potent masculinity.

He was driving a steel blue Mercedes tonight and the rich smell of leather enfolded her as she sank into the soft seat. He drove as he did most things, with a competent arrogance, showing a nicety of judgment and control which would have done credit to a Le Mans competitor. Some strong emotion roiled him—she could tell by the stiff set of his shoulders and the jut of his chin—but it didn't affect the smoothness of his reflexes. With a faint flicker of humor she decided that he wasn't used to anything less than enthusiastic acceptance of offers of his company and he wasn't finding the sensation pleasant or salubrious.

Perversely, the knowledge that she had annoyed him made Keri much more cheerful. She even leaned back against the seat and admired the burled wood fittings of the dashboard. It really was a very nice car. She ran a questing finger over the leather upholstery of the side panel nearest her and watched the lights of the city flow past outside the car window. A small, wholly feminine smile tugged at the corners of her mouth, and was duly noted by the man who wasn't looking at her, but nonetheless knew every move she made and every shade of expression which flitted across her face.

"Pleased with yourself, are you?" he spoke into the silence.

Keri debated internally for a fraction of a second and decided incomprehension was her safest course. "Pleased with myself?" she questioned quietly. "I'm afraid I don't understand."

"The butterfly has burst forth in glory. You're a lovely woman, Keri. It must be a relief to put away that childish masquerade and shed the drab skin. Was it fun playing dress-up, or in your case, dress-down?" There was a savage bite to the words which belied the even tone.

"Mr. Randolph, I began my masquerade as you term it, for good and sufficient reasons, the validity of which I still have no cause to doubt. I am sorry you were offended by my former appearance, but I was perfectly happy to remain Mr. Simonds's secretary. My appearance was a matter of indifference to him!" Keri was in a fine rage by the time she had finished the scathing words. By now she didn't care if he fired her on the spot.

Surprisingly, he laughed. "Calm down, little fireball," he advised her. "You're my secretary now and your appearance is not a matter of indifference to me. Just why did you begin this masquerade? I presume you didn't carry it over into your off-duty hours as well."

"No," she responded tautly. "It wasn't necessary. I

simply got tired of having to leave jobs because the boss thought it was fun to chase me around the desk." She shrugged slightly and continued. "So I asked my godfather, Charles Lawson, to find me a boss who looked at no woman but his wife and then I took steps to ensure that even if he looked a first time, he'd see nothing worth a second glance. It was an arrangement that suited both of us."

"Do you mean to tell me that Carleton Van Metre chased you around the desk?" he asked probingly.

Keri's face closed tightly. She didn't want to talk or even think about Schyler! "No," she admitted shortly. "I left Van Metre's for personal reasons which I have no intention of discussing, but they don't concern Mr. Carleton Van Metre except indirectly."

That blunt statement didn't seem to offend Dain, but he did let the subject drop, much to Keri's relief. It was bad enough to be hounded *by* Schyler. To be hounded *about* him too would be more than she was prepared to stand for. There was a taut set to Dain's mouth, but his next conversational gambit was merely to compliment her on the precision of her transcription of the meeting's notes and to thank her for the extra position summations and extraction of discussion points for easy reference.

By the time she had responded suitably, they had reached the hotel where the reception was to be held. The doorman assisted Keri from the car and another man took Dain's place behind the wheel to park the car. Dain drew Keri's hand through the crook of his elbow and held it there with the pressure of his covering hand. They mounted the steps together, a striking couple.

The manager came gliding forward to greet Dain and assure him that all was in perfect readiness. Keri was duly

69

introduced as one of Dain's secretaries as well as the hostess for the evening. She received the first of the speculative looks she had braced herself to endure. Knowing they were coming didn't make them any easier to take with equanimity.

The manager was a shade too effusive and he held on to Keri's hand a fraction too long, so her nod acknowledging the introduction was regally chill. In an effort to emphasize the formality of the relationship, she turned to Dain, whose narrowed eyes hadn't missed a bit of the byplay, and said, "Mr. Randolph, I would like to inspect the buffet and the placement of the flowers. I'm sure you and Mr. Garson will excuse me."

She was not to escape that easily. Dain grasped her hand again and inexorably drew it back to rest again in the crook of his arm. "We'll look over the arrangements together, Keri," he said firmly and drew her forward with him. Mr. Garson led the way obediently, sure now his first impressions were correct. The look he shot at Dain held more than a trace of envy.

Keri was exasperated. By subtle, cunning methods, which she was at a loss to know how to counteract, Dain Randolph was implying an intimacy between them. If he continued as he had begun, no one would have any doubts as to the quality of their relationship by evening's end. But how could she voice an objection to a possessive look or a simple courtesy which somehow assumed a proprietary air, without making herself look a hysterical idiot? A glance, a tone of voice . . . how best to fight their insidious impression?

Something in Dain's expression told her he recognized her dilemma and was amused by it . . . and would do nothing to extricate her.

They stood together to greet the first guests and from that beginning the reception followed the predictable pattern. Keri soon realized that many of the men hadn't made the initial connection between the machinelike secretary who had been present at the conference and the vivid woman who was propelled from group to group, willy-nilly, by Dain's pinioning arm, but some did, and they would spread the word to their less observant brethren.

Keri tried, time and time again, to slip away from the close confinement of Dain's hand at her waist, but found that unless she was prepared to make an obvious scene, her efforts were to no avail. She decided to bide her time. When the dancing started she would have her chance to escape him. As hostess she would have duty-dances with the principals of the conference and even the most determined Dain could not keep her at his side then. Cheered by that happy thought she could perform her duties graciously, a credit to her mother's tutelage.

The dancing started. The members of the conference claimed their duty-dances with flattering alacrity. By now they were all aware of her transformation and their reactions generally took one of two directions. Most, and they were the easiest to handle, took it as a joke, and while the heavy jocularity was wearying, it was far more welcome than the second reaction.

The second reaction was found among those of the group, a minority, fortunately, who perceived her new improved appearance as a come-on. Keri handled this group with a polite hauteur and blank incomprehension of their more suggestive innuendos. Unfortunately there were several, as there always are at every party, whose consumption of alcohol raised their spirits, lowered their inhibitions, and deafened them to any negative reaction short of one reinforced by a brickbat.

Keri caught Dain watching her several times as she did her best to preserve a neutral distance while dancing with one of this latter group. Anything less blatant than an outright knee to the groin hadn't a hope of getting through to Keri's current partner. When her eyes clashed with Dain's bland stare as she danced past, desperately trying to evade her partner's attempts to grind his hips against hers, Keri shot him a glare of such malignancy that her eyelashes should have smoked. He got her into this! She called down plagues and pestilence upon his head.

Her current partner swept her away, so she missed the black scowl that spread over Dain's face as he grimly watched the pair of retreating dancers. He divested himself of his own partner and within moments was skillfully cutting in on Keri and her overly enthusiastic and inebriated swain.

Although she currently viewed Dain in the same light as she would a case of shingles, at first Keri felt only relief. Dain held her lightly, if a trifle closely, but nothing compared to what she had been enduring. Her relief vanished like a snowflake in a blast furnace at his first words.

"Enjoying yourself, Keri? You seem to be the belle of the ball." His voice was as smooth as cream, but his eyes mocked openly.

Keri stiffened like a steel rod in his arms while her feet automatically kept pace with his expert lead. The face she lifted to his was calm, but her lips smiled nastily as she said pseudo-sweetly, "Of course, Mr. Randolph. I always enjoy being assaulted in public."

The music ended and she slipped out of his arms with a lithe twist. His hand went out to grasp her wrist but she had expected that he would try to recapture her and she evaded him neatly. For what remained of the evening she just as neatly avoided him. If he joined a group, she was just drifting away. She seemed to have eyes in the back of her head or some inner radar tuned just to warn of his approach. Had she been less deft it would have been farcical, but Keri was driven by sheer desperation. She didn't think her control could keep her from screaming at him like a fishwife and her pride shrank from the possibility of such a display.

She was also determined that she was not going to allow him to drive her home. She wasn't sure yet just how she was going to get out of it, but she'd maneuver. She had to!

A guardian angel, who had been soundly sleeping on some celestial cloud, finally woke up and got back on the job. The reception was nearly finished and Dain had at last managed to catch up with Keri. The last two groups of guests had coalesced into one, leaving her nowhere to run. Dain slipped an arm around her waist, pinning her to his side, and the bite of his fingers left her in no doubt that he meant to keep her there!

Salvation appeared in the unexpected form of two of the conference members who drew Dain aside for a lengthy conversation while Keri sped the last remaining guests out. The manager was hovering and Keri said, loudly enough for Dain to hear, "I would like to give our personal thanks to the hotel personnel in the kitchen, Mr. Garson. They have done an outstanding job tonight and have helped to make it a most successful party."

The manager proudly escorted her into the kitchen where Keri was sincere in her praise of the hotel staff's efforts. The pleased surprise told her that though RanCo often used this hotel's facilities for entertaining, evidently

Miss Barth had not deemed it necessary to render personal thanks before. Keri thought, a trifle cynically, Miss Barth might be surprised at the warmer "reception" she would get the next time she scheduled a function at this hotel. That had been one of the first lessons her mother had taught her about catered affairs. Always thank the kitchen workers personally.

The next step in her quickly formulated plan was easy to implement. She merely excused herself from Mr. Garson, saying that she would meet Mr. Randolph at the front desk after she had freshened up a bit.

She went to the front desk and left a message for Dain with the receptionist, the gist of which was that she had made her own way home by taxi since it was late and she didn't wish to take him out of his way. A warm smile at the doorman got her an instant taxi and she sank into the back seat, so different from the plush leather of her earlier conveyance, with overwhelming relief.

She figured that by the time Dain had retraced her trail through the hotel she would be well on her way home and so it proved true. She had been home nearly fifteen minutes before the knock came at the door. She'd taken the precaution of leaving the lights off everywhere except the bathroom, so there was nothing to betray her. He could assume she was home, but he couldn't prove it.

Five minutes after the knocking stopped, the phone started ringing. She didn't answer it either and after it stopped ringing the first time, she took it off the hook. He must have been calling from a nearby phone booth, but he didn't come back up and try his luck with the front door again. Once he started getting busy signals he'd *know* she was safely home, but she wanted an undisturbed night's sleep, and trying to ignore the ringing phone certainly wouldn't give it to her.

There was going to be hell to pay in more ways than one on Monday, but she comforted herself that she could always quit. With her typing speed she could turn out an error-free resignation letter in under one minute. Brief and to the point. An embassy job was looking more attractive by the minute. She'd been a nomad all her life. Maybe she shouldn't try to fight the system.

If she went to sleep on a downbeat, Keri awoke to an upbeat. Her natural optimism and sense of humor had both reasserted themselves during the night. Her job was challenging, the pay enticing, and she was tired of running. It was time to stand and fight.

But how? Well, to begin with, she decided, as she showered, she certainly wouldn't make the mistake she'd made with Schyler. There would be no dates with Dain Randolph, always assuming, of course, that he didn't fire her first thing on Monday morning. He couldn't force her to go out with him on a private basis. She didn't consider at the time that she might be outmaneuvered, and by her own emotions at that!

Buoyed by her resolution, she ate a hearty breakfast, pushed the phone button down for a moment to reestablish a connection, and dialed her godfather's number. When he answered she greeted him cheerfully. "Good morning to you, Charles. How'd you like to invite me to spend the weekend with you and Mary?"

"I'll tell Mary to put clean linens on your bed," was the satisfyingly prompt response. "Come when you can and stay as long as you can," he added.

"You're a love. I'll be there in time for lunch," she promised. After she had broken the connection, she left

75

the phone off the hook while she cleared away the break-fast dishes, packed her overnight bag, and flipped through her morning mail. She slipped several letters into her purse to read at her leisure, watered the philodendron and Boston fern, put the phone back on the hook, and headed toward the front door. The phone rang. She stuck her tongue out at it and closed the front door firmly behind her. She could hear its muted summons until the elevator door closed.

CHAPTER 4

True to her word, she reached the Lawsons' comfortable home in McLean, Virginia, by lunchtime. Charles, with exquisite diplomatic tact, didn't mention Schyler or RanCo at all as they ate their way through delicious tostadas. Mary had become addicted to Mexican cookery while she and Charles were with a diplomatic mission in Mexico City, and thereafter Mexican cuisine was featured regularly in her menus to the delight of her family and friends.

Keri helped with the dishes, grabbed a paperback she had started the previous weekend, and headed for the poolside. She pulled a lounger around to take maximum advantage of the sun, slathered herself with lotion, and dropped down gratefully onto the padded comfort of the sunwarmed canvas. There was a slight breeze to temper the heat of the sun and she read for a while in sybaritic comfort. Contented and relaxed as a cat, she surrendered to the soporific warmth of the afternoon as it dragged down her eyelids. The book fell unheeded to the ground and she dozed.

When she woke she was sticky with sweat and slightly heavy headed. The cool invitation of the pool seemed the ideal solution for both problems, and she ran lightly to the side, arcing into a racing dive without breaking stride. As she started her dive she caught a glimpse of two male figures approaching from around the side of the house. With the outline of their figures imprinted in her mind, she sliced cleanly into the water, breaking the smooth surface of the pool. She emerged, hair dripping in water-laden strands around her face, and turned to face the men. One was Charles. She sank slowly beneath the water again, trailing her floating, water-darkened hair behind her in a fan. The other was Dain Randolph.

Keri swam underwater toward the opposite end of the pool, surfacing under the diving board. She wondered, if she swam enough laps underwater, whether he'd give up and go away. Resignedly she decided he wouldn't. She submerged again and swam slowly back to the shallow end of the pool.

When she surfaced in the thigh-deep water Charles had gone back into the house and Dain stood by the steps, a towel waiting in his hand. Keri dipped back into the water to sleek her hair away from her eyes, wiped away the water drops caught in her eyelashes, and mounted the steps. He politely handed her the towel, which she draped casually around her shoulders after she had used it to mop her face.

Keri walked over to the lounger she had napped on so comfortably earlier and sat down. Her knees were tremulous and she quailed at the thin-lipped anger that pulled Dain's mouth. He looked very vital in the narrow-legged denims and pale green sport shirt which strained against the packed muscles of his legs and chest. In other circumstances she might have been pleasurably attracted by so much man. Just now though she wished him spindle-shanked and chicken-chested and anywhere but pushing her legs aside on the lounger so that he could sit down by her knees.

"Mr. Randolph," Keri said, with as cool an intonation as she could contrive, which frankly wasn't much, "this is a surprise." An eyebrow lifted in sardonic amusement at this massive piece of understatement, but lowered again when she unwisely continued, "Just passing by?"

Keri regretted this defensive bit of impudence as soon as it left her mouth, but it is hard to be coolly formal when dressed in a minuscule turquoise bikini and unexpectedly confronted by the devil on the doorstep, so to speak. With just a look he managed to make her feel gauche and vulnerable and it was all she could do not to huddle beneath the inadequate towel to hide herself from his stripping gaze.

He didn't speak and Keri fidgeted uneasily. Finally she could stand it no longer and once again blurted into unwise speech. "Did you come to fire me?"

"Do you think I should?" he countered easily, his face now an inscrutable mask, green eyes hooded against the glare of the afternoon sun.

Devil take the man, Keri thought in exasperation. *Just what do I answer to that? If I say yes, he just might take me at my word. If I say no, I give him the perfect opening.* She thought frantically and then temporized. "I would say that's up to you, sir," and reached down beside the lounger for her sunglasses, intending to put them on and hide behind their reflective blankness.

"Oh no you don't, Keri," he said as his hand snaked out

79

to encircle her wrist. "I've developed a distinct aversion to seeing you in glasses of any sort!" With his free hand he plucked the offending glasses from her fingers and placed them in the grass beneath the end of the lounge chair, safe but inaccessible to her.

Then, so suddenly that she started in amazement, his whole manner changed. He smiled at her with great charm and said quietly, "Shall we start over, Keri? I'll apologize for last night if you'll apologize for sneaking out after the reception. I could happily have wrung your neck, you know." Then he admitted casually, "You were probably very smart not to open the door or answer your phone until I had time to calm down."

Keri didn't answer his question directly at first. "How did you know I was with Charles and Mary for the weekend?" she asked bluntly.

"I called and asked to speak to you. Charles said you were dozing out by the pool, but that he'd go and get you. I told him not to wake you, that I'd contact you later, and so I have." He grinned at her.

It was hard not to answer his grin with her own, but she persevered. "But why did you think I might be here in the first place? I mean, I could just as easily have still been incommunicado at my apartment."

"I went by there," he said simply. "Your car was gone from its parking place and besides, you're not the type to stay holed up between four walls on a day like this. As to why the Lawsons . . . just luck. I knew of your relationship and took the chance that you might have come to them. Your mistake was in not telling them that you were hiding out from your boss."

"I wasn't hiding out!" she said indignantly.

He laughed at the absurdity of that assertion and Keri

could no longer hold out against the deliberately exerted charm. "And anyway, they don't know you're my boss yet. I hadn't told them that . . ."

"That I've pirated you away from Simonds?" he finished the sentence smoothly.

"Well, I was going to say transferred, but if you feel pirated fits better, I'll let you choose your own words." She smiled slightly at him in demure mischief, her green eyes glinting like bright glass from between the thick lashes.

"Pax, Keri?"

"Well, truce, Mr. Randolph," Keri assented cautiously. She still didn't trust him, but they had to establish some sort of ease between them if she were to continue at Ran-Co. She didn't deceive herself that he'd let her go back to work for Mr. Simonds. It was Dain Randolph or nothing. His manner made that clear.

"We're not in the office now, Keri. My name is Dain." He smiled when he said it, but it didn't lessen the authority behind the order.

Keri sighed. The truce was going to be of short duration. "Do your other secretaries call you Dain outside of the office?" She questioned him, avoiding using either Dain or Mr. Randolph.

"I don't see my other secretaries except in a business situation, Keri."

"Not even Miss Barth?" Keri couldn't resist.

"Especially not Miss Barth," he responded dryly. "Give me credit for a sense of self-preservation. I don't mix business with pleasure."

"Ah-ha!" Keri was triumphant. "Neither do I, Mr. Randolph."

"Very neat," he admitted, "but may I remind you that there are exceptions to the rule?"

"I know," Keri said bitterly, thinking of Schyler. "It's the exceptions that make me determined to stick to the rule from now on, Mr. Randolph."

"Which means that you won't let me take you out to dinner tonight." He said it as a statement, but there was a smile in his voice, as though something amused him. When she shook her head, he took her refusal calmly, merely saying, "What a shame. I had a particular craving for lobster tonight and there's an excellent seafood restaurant quite near here."

She looked up at him suspiciously, for he had risen as he spoke, but his face showed only polite regret. She started to rise as well, but he lightly touched her shoulder for a moment, arresting her motion. He broke the contact so that there was not the slightest presumption of intimacy, but she could feel that warm hand imprinted on her flesh long after he had gone.

"Don't get up, Keri. I'll manage to find my own way out. Enjoy your weekend."

He walked back to the house and she stared after him until he disappeared. She could have sworn he was laughing to himself.

She dived back into the pool and began to swim laps. A most disturbing episode. He was subtler than Schyler, but she didn't make the mistake of thinking him any the less determined. Unfortunately for her peace of mind, she also found Dain infinitely more attractive than she did Schyler!

She flipped over and floated on her back, considering the situation soberly. Superficially Dain and Schyler had much in common. Both were rich, experienced, and attractive. Inwardly she sensed a depth and strength of character in Dain that Schyler would never have. Both men might thus far have avoided lasting commitment to one woman, but in Dain there existed a capacity for deep, enduring emotion, even though it might never be utilized. Schyler had no such depths.

Keri's peril, as she saw it, would be the temptation to believe that she was the woman who could plumb those depths she sensed in Dain's character. As she turned over to finish the last lap and pulled herself up onto the edge of the pool she admitted too that she might come to believe it because she wanted to so badly. In spite of her common sense, in spite of Mrs. Covey's explicit details about Dain's previous women . . . she, Keri Dalton, idiot par excellence, would like very much to be that one woman. From the moment she had met those green eyes the first time in his office, something unexpected within herself had been unfolding and growing, and she was just now having to recognize and admit its existence. She wouldn't put a name to it yet, but neither could she deny its presence.

She wasn't ready to proffer explanations, so she avoided both Charles and Mary by going to her room to shower and shampoo the chlorine out of her hair. She dallied until the afternoon was well advanced and then, able to put it off no longer, went in search of her hosts. There were voices coming from the living room and she heard delighted laughter from Mary. She tracked the sound.

When she walked into the living room she knew why Dain had been laughing as he walked away from her. He sat at ease on the white couch, a long cool drink in his left hand, gesturing to illustrate a point with his right, while Mary sat beaming benignly at him from her favorite chair. Charles stood in his usual pose, back to the empty fireplace, arm cocked on the broad stone mantel, sipping occasionally from his own drink.

Dain rose as she entered the room and the look he shot her was as mischievous as any small boy's. "Charles and Mary like lobster too, Keri," he said significantly and couldn't have looked more pleased with himself if he'd turned into a pillar of smug.

Keri looked interrogatively at Mary, who smiled guilelessly back at her and said happily, "Dain says he knows of a good restaurant near here that specializes in fresh lobster and he's invited us all to have dinner with him. Isn't that nice of him, dear? You know how I enjoy lobster, and it's quite Charles's favorite food."

Keri looked over at Dain. His eyes danced with unholy glee and invited her to laugh with him at the ease with which he had circumvented her. A reckless streak surfaced (it had gotten her into trouble before) and she succumbed to temptation. She laughed. It was the husky chuckle of a clear brook over water-smooth rocks, innocent and sparkling, bubbling with joy. Something flamed deeply in Dain's eyes before he drooped his lids to shield what could be read there.

Mary regarded Keri with some confusion and Charles questioned dryly, "Is this a private joke or may anyone join in?" It had been far too long since he had heard Keri laugh with all her old zest and he was most curious to discover just what triggered that enchanting gurgle of mirth.

"I've been neatly outmaneuvered, Charles," Keri admitted, laughter still lilting in her voice. "Meet my boss, Dain Randolph. He pirated"—she grinned with an urchin's cheeky impudence at Dain,—"me away from my cozy Mr. Simonds and pried me out of my depressive disguise. Now he's managed to vanquish my resolutions about not mixing my business life with pleasure, for tonight, at least."

"Hostilities to recommence on Monday, Keri?" Dain drawled in amusement.

"What's wrong with Sunday?" she shot back, eyes sparkling.

"Sunday is a day of rest," he intoned pontifically, sending Keri off into another gust of mirth. Dain grinned back and suddenly there was a flashing sense of conspiracy, as though the two of them shared a joke no one else could understand. Days later Keri was to realize that the joke, if one could call it that, was on her, but by then it was far, far too late.

Dain exerted himself to please, and he did it well, Keri had to admit grudgingly. He didn't display the practiced charm of Schyler, which had always rung slightly forced and shopworn to her critical ear. Dain simply set his guests at ease, smoothing away the tension and wary regard that emanated from the guest who sat beside him in the booth, facing Charles and Mary.

He kept a proper distance from her, not taking advantage of the fact that she was captive between him and the wall, but even while talking to the opposite couple she was all too conscious of his proximity. By turning her head fractionally she could observe the hard outline of his profile and the determined thrust of his jaw. He was a man accustomed to decision-making, who would be ruthless if he saw the need. She judged he could be a good friend and a very bad enemy, but she doubted that he had any women who were merely friends. Platonic relationships, from what Mrs. Covey had told her and what she deduced herself from his experienced eyes and sensually firm mouth, would have little interest for him.

He was fascinating and dangerous. She'd be a fool to think she could escape unscathed from any relationship with him save the most cursory and formal and he'd already made it clear that their future relationship wasn't going to be either cursory or formal. She'd be safer picking up a live high-voltage wire in her bare hands than she would be picking up the challenge Dain had thrown her. Keri glanced sideways at Dain only to have her gaze collide and lock with his as his eyes lifted from an unhurried study of her profile.

Excitement warred with prudence and prudence sank without a trace. Keri let a slow, almost feline smile curve her lips, green eyes tilting at the corners as a perceptible vivid excitement bloomed on her expressive face. She watched Dain suck in an involuntary gasp as she bathed him with the full force of her smile and gaze. Just because she had heretofore avoided using feminine wiles didn't mean she didn't know how to use them when it suited her! Perhaps attack might turn out to be the best defense after all.

The remainder of the evening was brilliant with rapid fire repartee. Charles and Mary swiveled like spectators at a tennis match when Keri threw away all remnants of her protective quietude and flamed with an almost febrile gaiety. If her previous tactics of avoidance had piqued Dain's interest, perhaps a complete reversal of strategy was called for.

Secure in the knowledge that Dain couldn't possibly do anything to her in Charles and Mary's protective presence, she sidled closer to him in the booth and proceeded to give a consummate imitation of a moth being drawn helplessly toward an engulfing flame. Charles, who knew his goddaughter very well, enjoyed the performance tremendously.

While they waited for their lobster to be served, Keri allowed her bare arm to brush against Dain's as she reached for her water glass. She sipped slowly and replaced the glass in the same place. Somehow Dain's arm had moved imperceptibly closer and the contact was firmer the second time. Keri grinned inwardly. There were no lost opportunities allowed around Dain!

She turned a gravely worshipful face up to his and fired a broadside. "It was so thoughtful of you to take us out for dinner tonight, Dain." She delicately laid only the faintest, breathy emphasis on the Dain. "It's rare for a girl to find such a considerate employer, but it really wasn't necessary, you know." She lectured gently. "The duties expected from an executive's secretary are quite a bit more comprehensive than those required from a typist in the typing pool, and acting as hostess for a business function certainly falls well within the scope of secretarial responsibilities! I'm perfectly willing to perform all my secretarial duties without additional reward." She fluttered her eyelashes at him outrageously.

Without hesitating a beat she turned to face Charles and Mary, and continued confidingly. "Dain has just finished an exhausting round of negotiations and last night RanCo held a party for the participants to celebrate the successful conclusion and signing of contracts. I was so happy to be able to help out when Dain asked me to act as his hostess. These contracts were quite a coup for RanCo."

The wide-eyed ingenuity of her look and dulcet demureness in her voice caused Charles and Dain to choke slightly as they took simultaneous sips of their drinks, but Mary beamed proudly at her goddaughter.

"I know Dain realizes just how fortunate he is to have you as his secretary, Keri, dear. Too many young girls nowadays don't realize that loyalty to an employer requires more than a strict nine-to-five workday at times. When I think of some of the secretaries Charles has had to contend with . . . well, really. Some of them couldn't even take down a telephone message correctly." Mary essayed a small joke. "You can take them down in six languages."

Keri chuckled. She glanced mischievously at Dain and added an outrageous postscript. "I'm sure Dain realizes *exactly* what kind of secretary he has working for him."

Fortunately for Keri the lobsters arrived at the table, because the glint in Dain's eyes was assuming rapier-sharp intensity. As she lifted a butter-dripping bite of lobster to her lips, Keri caught Charles's glance and he shook his head slightly in amused admonition. She returned the look he had seen all too often on her face when she was accepting some reckless dare from her older brothers, designed to prove she could do whatever it was just as well as they could! The proving had every so often cost her some bruises and once a broken bone, but it had never quenched her zest for a challenge. Headstrong as she was, but generally not reckless to a fault, he hoped Keri wasn't getting herself into a situation where she risked more being broken than a bone.

To say that having the tables turned on him was a novel experience for Dain was to understate the situation. Instead of running away from him, Keri now seemed to be running full tilt directly at him, on a collision course, in fact. Her glances were arch and her words provocative and the drift of her perfume in his nostrils was as teasing as the occasional warm brush of her arm and thigh. After those first lightly barbed thrusts, Keri settled down to conduct a serious flirtation.

With innate skill, learned at numerous embassy functions, she drew him out, had him doing all the talking before he realized what was happening. He was bemused by enormous green eyes and softly pouting lips. A slow smile made an elusive dimple flick in and out of her cheek and a soft touch of her hand and an admiring look increased his eloquence whenever it seemed to falter. Keri was careful to draw Charles and Mary into the admiring circle, a task made easy because Dain was genuinely interesting.

In normal circumstances Dain was habitually reserved, a past master at encouraging others to talk while he listened. His business caution reinforced a natural reticence, and though he could be an amusing raconteur, he gave little away of his personal feelings. He was a very private man, but Keri skillfully unlocked the guarded areas of his personal opinions, illuminating the real Dain Randolph to a degree his business associates would have found astounding.

When Dain was released from the enchantment, after he had dropped Keri, Charles, and Mary at their home, he realized with a shock just how deftly he had been interrogated. Keri had asked him nothing damaging, but he wasn't at all sure that he wouldn't have spilled out secrets with the fluidity of a waterfall if she had formed the questions with those enticing lips and snared him with those silky soft eyelashes.

She had promised all evening, but she made him forget to ask her to deliver, and he had meekly escorted her to her godparents' front door with all the respectful rectitude of a Victorian suitor. She had hidden more than physical beauty beneath that prim, deceptive exterior, and when he had released that glorious hair from the confinement of its beauty-destroying bun, it seemed that he had also unfettered a devious and mischievous mind. In short, she had taken him for an unexpected ride and he was just starting to realize how far off course she'd steered him.

As for Keri, when she finally lay in bed that night in Charles and Mary's guest room, she wondered how she'd dared. It had seemed like such a good idea at the time, and Dain's reaction to her fledgling, trial run at being a femme fatale had been supremely satisfying, but *what* was she going to do for an encore? She certainly wasn't going to pay off on all those promises she'd made him from the security of Charles and Mary's chaperonage. He now probably figured she was the hottest thing since jalapeños were invented. He certainly hadn't run fast and furiously in the other direction from a pursuing female, to wit, herself, and she was dreadfully afraid that instead of finding his thrills by pursuing an unwilling female, Dain was looking forward to enjoying her pursuit of him! That was all wrong, and certainly not according to her plan. What would she *do* with him if she caught him?

She had a naturally optimistic nature, so her sleep was deep and refreshing, but her subconscious must have slept well too because it didn't present her with a tidy solution to Dain when she woke up the next morning. Keri lay in bed stretching and considering. All in all, Monday was going to be an uncomfortable day, caught as she would be between Miss Barth's jealous incredulity and Dain's expectations. She briefly considered what would happen if she remained the old Miss Dalton in defiance of Dain's orders, but decided that she could cope better with Miss Barth than she could with an infuriated Dain. He was going to be angry about being led down the garden path as it was. Not smart to add insult to insult.

Fortunately for Keri, Sunday passed peacefully. She accompanied her godparents to church and to lunch afterward. Charles and Mary had made plans to visit a friend recovering from an operation, and their relationship with Keri was so comfortably close that there was no strain on either side when they left her to fend for herself for the afternoon. She found herself free to spend the time drowsing by their pool, deepening her tan, and finally finishing the book she had started. The phone rang twice and she ignored it both times, on the theory that if it were for her godparents they wouldn't have been home to answer it anyway, and if it were for her it would most assuredly be Dain and she didn't want to talk to him.

She had a light supper ready by the time Charles and Mary returned and they spent the rest of the evening in quiet companionship. Keri shared her latest letter from her parents and the news from her two brothers, one of whom was a mining engineer on a job in Canada while the other built bridges in South America. Charles and Mary had two children, both of whom were doctors, and they reciprocated with the latest adventures of Charles, Jr., and Steve. Mary also made her usual comment at this time, to the effect that she had always hoped that Keri and Steve . . . allowing the phrase to die gently away. Keri responded tolerantly that she loved Steve like a brother, which she did, but wouldn't have him as a husband even to get the two best in-laws a girl could ever want. He was a pathologist who liked to talk shop, a failing even a doting mother had to agree was a drawback to serene mealtimes.

* * *

Keri crept back into her apartment building with all the stealth of a seasoned burglar. Instead of coming openly up the elevator, she scurried up the fire stairs and peeked around the shielding door before venturing out into the corridor leading to her apartment. She felt rather foolish when the corridor proved innocent of any looming male figures, but reasoned foolish was better than caught. She just wasn't in the mood for a confrontation between herself and either Schyler or Dain. Tomorrow was going to be upsetting enough, if she read Miss Barth right, and she preferred not to dissipate her energies beforehand.

The next morning Keri searched among her pre-disguise-days wardrobe for her most becoming work outfit. It was a tailored suit, but bore no resemblance whatsoever to the suit she had worn the previous Friday. It was a clear, soft forest green and faithfully reflected the curved body beneath it. The soft silky blouse of cream and green lay smoothly against her skin. Her hair was pulled away from her face, but tumbled in a shining flow down the back of her neck. The prim Miss Dalton had vanished, basically unlamented, leaving behind the Keri of old.

This time, when she drove to work, her car matched her appearance and she got the first reaction to her new image after she deftly slid it into her assigned parking spot. As she locked the car she noticed two of the girls from the typing pool walk by on their way into the building, and as they saw her standing by her car, Keri received her first double take of the day. The stammered "Good morning, Miss Dalton?" with its rising inflection caused Keri's lips to twitch, her unruly sense of humor nearly getting the best of her. It would not have been kind to laugh, nor

92

polite, but it was a near thing. Their faces were most expressive.

Keri dropped her key into her purse, allowing the two to gain a respectable distance from her. No sense in unduly inhibiting their discussion of her! She seemed oblivious to the covert glances cast back over their shoulders as she strolled in a leisurely fashion behind them, and they sped up, eager to carry the news of the miraculous transformation.

Keri didn't know whether to hope that the news would filter ahead of her, rising like the flood of high tide, to the executive level. Would Miss Barth be forewarned and therefore forearmed? On the whole, Keri rather spitefully hoped that Miss Barth wouldn't hear beforehand. The look on her face when confronted by the new Keri was probably going to be the only funny part of the day.

So many double takes followed Keri's progress to the elevator that she wondered if the company was going to get a rash of whiplash complaints at the infirmary. She was beginning to get irritated. Damn Dain Randolph anyway. She could have made the transformation gradually if he'd let her, and she wouldn't now feel as though she were the star attraction at a freak show.

When she stalked into the suite of offices used by Dain, Keri knew she had her wish. Miss Barth hadn't heard. She was standing close to Dain as he gave her instructions, evidently concerning a report he held in his hand, but Keri sensed that the report was merely window dressing. Dain was there to see if she had obeyed his orders, and from the way his eyes flickered from Keri, confirming her appearance, back to watch Miss Barth, Keri knew he had wanted to be on hand to see Miss Barth's reaction. It was worth watching, if you liked that sort of thing.

It certainly was classic. Miss Barth's mouth dropped open, her eyes widened and darkened with shock. She turned white, then red, then white again around the mouth and nostrils, her shiny red lipgloss standing out starkly against the surrounding pressure-whitened skin. It gave the momentary effect of a clown mask—scarlet mouth against white greasepaint,—but it wasn't a smile that twisted those lips.

All humor had fled from the situation as far as Keri was concerned. She had made an enemy, though not by her will or by her desire. Miss Barth was feeling a fool and she was sure to blame Keri, human nature being sadly what it is.

"Ah, good morning, Miss Dalton." Dain's smoothly appreciative voice unfroze the three of them. "How charming you look this morning. A new outfit?"

Keri shot him a malignant glare. Somehow she knew that he'd never commented on Miss Barth's attire, new or not, and was merely pouring gasoline instead of soothing oil on inflammable and troubled waters! He didn't wither suitably beneath her scorning glare and his mouth compressed and twitched suspiciously.

Keri tried to salvage what she could of the situation. She ignored his comment. "Good morning, Mr. Randolph. Good morning, Miss Barth. I hope you had a pleasant weekend, Miss Barth."

Miss Barth didn't answer. No matter how exciting her weekend had been, Keri had just ruined her day!

"*I* had a very nice weekend, Miss Dalton," Dain introjected smoothly. Keri waited for his next words with a sense of inescapable fatalism. He was going to . . . He did. "I found your godparents charming, and I'm glad they

94

enjoyed our dinner together. We'll have to take them out again soon, won't we?"

Keri's look assured him that she'd see him served up as the main course, an apple stuffed firmly in his mouth, if they ever dined together again. Miss Barth was oblivious to the byplay and Keri's disinclination to attract Dain's notice. As far as she was concerned, Keri Dalton was a scheming, manchasing, unprincipled epithet and the sooner she, Elise Barth, made Keri's position untenable, the better.

Keri glanced briefly at Miss Barth and read her mind like an open book. *Oh, Mr. Simonds,* she lamented mentally. *Why did you ever have to mention that you had a new secretary?* Keri still suffered under the delusion that Dain had heard of her through normal channels. Her enlightenment on that misconception was in the mercifully still shrouded future.

Feeling that nothing more could be gained, Keri prepared to retreat into the relative safety of the office she shared with Mrs. Covey. At least that lady wouldn't look at her with the hungry ferocity of a starving vixen preparing to take the first bite out of a farmyard chicken. Miss Barth's eyes had lost their initial dark surprise and now glittered with an icy malice, the pupils contracted to pinpoints of antagonism.

"If you'll excuse me, Mr. Randolph—"Keri began, moving toward the door. She wasn't allowed to finish.

"Just a moment, Keri." Her eyes flashed to him in shock. This was really going too far. Miss Barth's mouth had fallen open again. "I'd like to see you in my office for a moment, Keri. I have a few things I wish to discuss with you that I wasn't able to cover on Sunday." His look was significant and compelling.

Keri knew then, without further confirmation, that it had been Dain on Sunday, letting the phone peal in those demanding summons which she had so determinedly ignored. She knew too, that he suspected, though he couldn't prove it without interrogating Charles and Mary, that she had been avoiding him. His phrasing was also deliberately designed to leave Miss Barth free to speculate just what they *had* covered on Sunday.

With scant regard for business protocol Keri tramped past Dain and into his office, leaving him to follow behind. As soon as he came in and closed the door behind them, she whirled on him, ready to do battle.

"*Mr.* Randolph, I do not appreciate the impression you have managed to give Miss Barth, that I am . . . that we are . . ." she floundered, searching for the *mot juste*.

He watched her struggles with amusement, but declined to supply any suitable word from his no doubt extensive vocabulary. Finally Keri was able to stop sputtering and express herself in coherent English.

She said stiffly, "I am your employee, Mr. Randolph, your secretary. I would appreciate it if you would cease implying that I am anything more. Friday night you implied, none too subtly I might add, that I was more than your secretary, and now, in front of Miss Barth, you implied that we . . . we . . ." Here Keri ran into word trouble again. ". . . that you and I are on such terms that we dine with my relatives," she finished bitterly.

"Didn't I dine with your relatives?" he asked mockingly.

"Oh, yes, but only because you sneakily contrived it. You *knew* I didn't want to go out with you," she accused him.

He fixed her with a kindling eye. He could only keep an

96

upper hand with this infuriating woman if he kept his temper, but it was going to be a hard thing to do. "Didn't you have a good time after I dragooned you into going?" he asked her in a silkily dangerous tone.

"That's beside the point!" Keri was determined not to give an inch.

"That's exactly the point," he flashed back. "And here's another point, Keri. I *am* the boss. This office will be run in the manner I dictate. If I want to call you by your first name, I will, and you'd better answer to it."

By now Dain had advanced from his position by the door to loom over Keri as she stood backed up by his desk. She could feel the edge cutting into the soft flesh of her thighs. She couldn't retreat any farther and still he came closer, until they were nearly touching and she had to strain her neck to look up and meet his eyes. Like her own, his green eyes glittered with suppressed emotion and for a moment the primitive man showed through.

He glared at her for a long moment and then stepped back, giving her a clear path to the door. "Get out of here, Keri. Run back to your nice safe office. You might have shed the exterior Miss Prim, but her soul still lurks underneath!"

"Nice safe office, huh!" Keri muttered as she closed the door behind her not quite in a slam. "I may have been delivered from the lion's den for the moment, but the lady jackal is lurking just outside."

She hoped she didn't look as distraught as she felt inside. Miss Barth would be sure to dive straight for the jugular at the slightest sign of weakness. A bland, imperturbable facade against which Miss Barth would blunt her fangs and the comforting alternative of an embassy job

somewhere on the other side of the world would be her
shield and buckler.

CHAPTER 5

By the end of the day Keri wished instead for an armored tank. Miss Barth's unsubtle spray of venom had eaten numerous holes in her "imperturbable" facade and Keri didn't believe that there was an embassy or even a legation in Antarctica, which is where she most longed to be at the moment.

As she had expected fatalistically, Miss Barth was lying in wait just outside Dain's door. When Keri emerged from the ogre's den, Miss Barth pounced, and her first bite was no mere nip at the heels.

"Well, Miss Dalton, what a transformation! Decided that there are faster ways to advancement than through merit, have you?"

Keri fought back a retort in kind—several searing ones jostled to be first out of her mouth—and merely stared frostily at the hostile woman. It lacked the quelling authority of her previous stares since this one was no longer backed up by her matching Miss Prim persona, but evi dently it still carried enough force to shift Miss Barth back out of Keri's line of progress. Keri swept into her own office and shut the door firmly behind her. She leaned weakly back against the comforting solidity of the door, her eyes closed while she struggled to master her rampaging emotions.

"Elise makes a bad friend and a worse enemy." The dry comment snapped Keri's eyes open. Mrs. Covey regarded her from her desk, a sympathetic smile creasing the plump folds of her cheeks. "Don't worry, Keri. You're more than a match for Elise at her worst." She surveyed Keri judiciously. "For one thing, you've got better equipment than she has."

Keri groaned heartrendingly. "Mrs. Covey, you are definitely Job's comforter right now. My equipment, as you call it, is what's gotten me into this mess." She raised her hands theatrically to heaven. "All I asked for was a simple secretarial job, where nobody noticed me and I could do my work without all of these brangles. A peaceful life, a simple life . . . was it too much to ask?" Heaven didn't bother to answer, and Keri dropped her hands to her sides. Humor had surfaced and Keri was back on balance. The friendly exchange with Mrs. Covey had restored her equilibrium and she could begin to put the morning's events into some sort of perspective. If only she would be left alone for the rest of the day to strengthen her fragile composure.

Keri got her wish, for the rest of the morning at least. She and Mrs. Covey were deeply immersed in the complexities of the report concerning the latest takeover, assembling, ordering, and translating the relevant papers into a comprehensive and tidy whole.

Whenever further material was needed, Mrs. Covey

tactfully sallied forth to gather the requisite pieces of paper. She kindly didn't tell Keri about the increased traffic Elise was having to deal with. There seemed to be a steady stream of people with spurious excuses who came, hoping to confirm the rumor of Miss Dalton's miraculous transformation into a femme fatale. Opportunistic young executives hovered like honeybees, but it wasn't Miss Barth's nectar they wished to sip.

Dain erupted in the middle of one gathering of drones. He had flashed twice for Miss Barth, and receiving no immediate response (an unprecedented event, since she usually appeared before he had time to take his finger off the summoning button!), he came out to investigate.

Unlike Keri, Dain's temper was still simmering, and the hapless young executives received a sizable portion of the nicely boiling ire. Dain took in the gathering with a comprehensive glance and understood its origin and intent in an instant. It didn't help his temper to know that word of Keri's transformation had spread so rapidly and with such devastating results.

"Well, gentlemen?" He surveyed the hovering men with cold green eyes. "Have you come in a delegation to see me about some crisis which threatens RanCo? It must indeed be critical to find so many of the brightest of our executive crop ungainfully employed." The gathering nearly teleported away, so swift was the dispersal. Fortunately no one was crushed in the effort to be first through the office door.

Mrs. Covey, legitimately employed in gathering more material, had stood well away from the dangerous path of egress. She continued to dawdle unobtrusively so she could witness the final scene. It was a dilly.

"And now, Miss Barth," Dain snarled silkily, "*if* you

would be so kind. I have some letters which are urgent. Since your hovering court has dispersed, perhaps now you will find time to concentrate on the work you were hired to do." He stood waiting for the white-faced Miss Barth to gather her materials together and then ushered her within the inner sanctum with exaggerated courtesy.

Well, that's the first time ever that Elise won't enjoy being alone with Dain Randolph, Mrs. Covey observed to herself. *Elise won't even wait to get Keri alone in a dark alley after this.* She clutched her papers to her ample bosom and went back into her own and Keri's office.

Mrs. Covey didn't mention the scene in the outer office, but when lunchtime arrived, she suggested that she and Keri once again forgo the company cafeteria and eat away from the premises of RanCo. Keri, restored by the morning of uninterrupted paperwork, demurred at first.

"I'll have to face them sometime, Mrs. Covey. I might as well get it over with," she offered bravely. "I had a sample of the reaction when I came up to the office this morning. It'll all die down if I just ignore it."

"I don't know if you'll be able to ignore it, Keri," Mrs. Covey confessed soberly. She went on to detail the morning's events and concluded, "Elise will really have her knives out for you now. Dain Randolph has never spoken to her that way before and she's sure to blame you. She has a coterie of friends who follow her lead slavishly and if those harpies start in on you, Custer's last stand will be a Sunday picnic by comparison."

Keri's eyes began to flash. "Perhaps an unfortunate simile for Miss Barth. She can't be sure she'll end up on the side of the Indians. Custer had blond hair, and though Elise Barth's is bleached to that color, the principle may turn out to be the same. I believe the menu of the cafeteria features cabbage rolls today, Mrs. Covey. They're one of my favorite dishes and I'd hate to miss a chance to try the cafeteria's version of them. Shall we go?"

The outer office was deserted. The two women escaped to the hall without incident and then traded a conspiratorial glance. They didn't know where Elise was, perhaps still closeted with Dain, but at least she hadn't been glaring at them from behind her desk!

The next stop was the rest room, where Keri gilded the lily with fresh lipgloss and a swift hairbrush through her auburn mop. Her eyes glittered green without further enhancement and nothing was needed to tilt her chin into a determined slant. Mrs. Covey decided privately that if she were a betting woman, which, regretfully she wasn't, she'd put a hefty bet on Keri.

Keri slipped her shoulderbag over her arm and with Mrs. Covey in tow, sailed into the cafeteria. To say that all conversation ceased when they entered would be incorrect, but there was a noticeable drop in the sound level of the hum of voices and a rippling effect, much like that of wind through a grain field, as heads turned to follow Keri's progress toward the steam tables.

After the initial lowering of conversation, the increased volume was all the more noticeable. Keri seemed oblivious to it all, but Mrs. Covey observed that the fingers that grasped her tray were white from the pressure she was exerting. She smiled pleasantly at the woman who served her plate with the requested cabbage rolls, and Mrs. Covey noticed that Keri got an extra helping of tomato sauce over her selection. Subtle sympathy?

Keri seemed unaware of the wave of interest her appearance had spawned, but as Mrs. Covey so cannily observed, it was surface serenity only. Her stomach churned and her face felt stiff as she forced her expression into self-possessed impassivity. She wanted to scream at all the staring eyes, *Stop looking at me! It's not my fault. Your precious boss got me into this.*

Not a hint of the inner turmoil appeared, however, and as they paused by the cashier after paying for their meals, both women surveyed the room for space to sit. Keri saw Elise and a group of friends sitting across the room, heads together, but darting glances at Keri between whispered comments. Mrs. Covey had spotted a table for two on the opposite side of the room and she directed Keri's attention toward it, but Keri had decided to carry the attack to the enemy. There was also an empty table right next to Elise and her comrades. Keri headed toward it, with Mrs. Covey gamely bringing up the rear.

Keri took the seat which faced outward into the room and which not so incidentally placed her directly in line with Elise. Keri nodded regally to Elise and received a blistering glare in return. A besetting sense of mischief overtook Keri and she smiled sweetly. Elise was taken aback and momentarily flustered. Hot color, due mostly to fury, ran up under the skin of her cheeks, tinting her makeup a momentary blotched orange. The clown mask of rage reappeared, but Keri faced her opponent guilelessly until Elise turned away and broke the eye contact, disconcerted.

Keri then began to eat her cabbage rolls with every evidence of enjoyment. She and Elise were never going to be friends, but Elise was going to respect her as an opponent or Keri would know the reason why! She cut into a cabbage roll with savage precision.

"I think Elise would like to hand you a salt shaker full

104

of ground glass right now," Mrs. Covey commented with understated perceptiveness.

"Just at this moment, I could probably eat it and come to no harm," Keri retorted. "If I could shake it over Dain Randolph's heart I'd probably even relish it!" She glanced up from her plate, checking on Elise's whereabouts, but the other woman was avoiding her eye. Keri returned her attention to her own lunch.

"So you'd like his heart on a plate, would you?" Mrs. Covey chuckled.

"I wouldn't have any part of him on a silver platter," Keri shot back, but she grinned wryly and added, "and don't quote me the one about the lady doth protest too much. That's always seemed to me to be a singularly irritating quotation and as unfair as the old have-you-stopped-beating-your-wife question. You can't win either way."

By now both women were into dessert and Keri watched Elise and her friends gather up their trays, preparing to depart. Elise's and Keri's eyes met once again, and as before, Elise's eyes fell first. Keri watched her walk away, stiff-backed and bristling, and knew that life in the executive complex was going to be dicey for a long time to come. She mentally shrugged with resigned acceptance. It was all so futile—she would have happily and, at this moment, truthfully reassured Elise about her lack of designs on their mutual boss—but Elise was unable to believe in Keri's innocence of intent or to accept the even more unpalatable fact that with or without Keri's attractive presence, Elise Barth had no chance with Dain Randolph anyway. Elise had had three years to make what headway she could and she was still Miss Barth, both in

105

public and in private. Unfortunately for Keri, Elise Barth was not a graceful loser.

Keri began to get the first intimations of just how ungracious a loser Elise was when she and Mrs. Covey overheard one of Elise's friends regaling a group of typists waiting for the elevators with Elise's accusation, suitably embellished, that Keri had her sights set on being something more than a secretary to Dain Randolph, and that something wasn't a wife. Dain's wife, when he acquired one, would of course come from that exalted strata of Society to which the Randolph name gave entree. Keri, however, would be satisfied to aim for a slightly lower and less permanent position, if, it was spitefully added, she hadn't attained it already!

Mrs. Covey gasped in outrage and the sound brought the group's attention to the newly arrived pair. Keri was almost rigid with blazing wrath, but she clove easily through the appalled group to confront the petrified woman who was Elise's crony. Keri was indeed a daunting sight, but her voice, when it came, was almost caressingly soft.

"Have you ever been sued for slander, Miss Thurston? I can guarantee that it is an experience that you not only wouldn't enjoy but couldn't afford. I don't hold my reputation lightly and neither does my father, General Dalton, nor my godfather, Ambassador Lawson. You might pass the word to your friends that should I hear further filth of this sort, you'll be given a chance to repeat it and substantiate it from the witness stand in a courtroom, with Barnabas Tolson asking you the pertinent questions. He's known me and my family all of my life and he thinks highly of my reputation too."

The elevator arrived at the psychological moment and

Keri and Mrs. Covey stepped into it, to ride up in solitary splendor since not one of the stunned women in the group was capable of moving a muscle. Keri was drawing deep breaths in an attempt to calm herself before she went into the office and figuratively and perhaps literally tore Elise Barth into tiny little particles.

"Do you really know Barnabas Tolson?" Mrs. Covey questioned in awe. He was one of the foremost criminal lawyers in the nation, and his cross-examinations were deadly.

"He was my father's roommate at West Point," Keri answered absently, still intent on calming herself back into coherence. "He's godfather to my oldest brother, and my dad's godfather to his daughter."

The elevator traveled upward in silence after that revelation. When it reached their floor, Keri strode out of the elevator as soon as the doors had slid back the mere width of her body. Mrs. Covey wasn't as quick off the mark, but she reached Elise's office scant seconds after Keri did. Mrs. Covey couldn't see Keri's face, but she could see Elise's and she watched the color drain from the seated woman's complexion.

"Would you like to step into my office, Elise, or shall we have it out right here?" Keri's voice still carried those caressing overtones it had held when she had peeled the skin off Miss Thurston ten floors below. Elise's mouth opened and closed soundlessly and she gasped for breath through a constricted throat.

Keri walked over to the inner door, leading to their shared office, and said gently to Mrs. Covey, "Would you take over for Elise for a few minutes? She and I have some unfinished business to discuss."

Mrs. Covey moved obediently toward Elise's desk as the

other woman rose jerkily to her feet and walked into the inner office with the precision of an automaton. Keri waited until Elise had passed through and then followed her, shutting the door softly behind them both.

Keri turned away from the closed door and regarded Elise as she stood defiantly by Mrs. Covey's desk. She let the silence stretch ominously until Elise had swallowed heavily twice and shifted her feet restlessly. Then Keri spoke.

"You are a very stupid woman, Elise. You've put yourself into an untenable position. You're out on a limb and I'm just about to saw it off behind you. I had and have no designs on Dain Randolph, but whether I have or not is no concern of yours. I was prepared to put up with petty spite from you as long as you kept it confined to the office, but I am not prepared to put up with slander, in or out of the office. I've already served notice to your friend, Miss Thurston, that if you and she and any other of your pals continue to perpetrate that tissue of scurrilous innuendo you dreamed up, I'll strip you naked financially and emotionally with a suit for slander that will leave you without a shred of reputation yourself. You won't even be able to get a job as a waitress in a Skid Row bar, much less as an executive secretary." She watched the emotions flit restlessly across the pale woman's face before continuing in that same gentle tone. "Don't make the mistake of thinking I'm bluffing. Barnabas Tolson doesn't bluff and he's my brother's godfather and a lifelong friend of my family."

Keri watched the woman facing her sway slightly, but Keri's green eyes remained merciless. "Don't faint yet, Elise," she advised in a controlled voice. "There's still more to come. Your poison has had time to spread already, thanks to those of your friends who wouldn't have gotten the word from Miss Thurston yet, so you'll have to go to work to repair the damage you've caused. You'd better contact every one of them and convince them to spread further word that it was spite, not fact, that formed the basis of your previous fabrication, and that you deeply regret the whole incident."

Elise moved protestingly, but Keri wasn't finished with her, and that steady, contemptuous green gaze held her impaled. "You'd better pray also that Mr. Randolph doesn't get wind of this little episode. I don't think he'd take too kindly to your efforts to blacken the reputation of a woman you think he's interested in."

Elise's face went even whiter, a feat Keri had thought impossible. This aspect of the situation had clearly never occurred to Elise and contemplation of it scared her as much as the threat of Barnabas Tolson. Keri was satisfied. Elise might be stupid in some ways, but she had a healthy sense of survival. There would be no further trouble from her.

Keri moved away from the door and opened it invitingly. Elise still hadn't said a word, but she obediently walked toward the outer office, only too glad to get away from that emerald-eyed witch. Prim Miss Dalton had concealed the fighting abilities of a Tasmanian devil and Elise was bleeding from a thousand invisible wounds. She walked into her office and sank into the chair which Mrs. Covey had vacated when the door opened. She buried her face in shaking hands and contemplated the wreck of her future.

Keri had crossed to her own desk and her legs were as trembly as Elise's. Reaction was setting in and she felt sick to her stomach. Anger had carried her through the dreadful scenes, but now the adrenaline flow was ebbing and a

109

churning nausea rose, bile-bitter in her throat. Malice, active malicious spite, is never pleasant, and when turned against oneself it sickens and wounds. She wished she could go home and take a long hot cleansing shower. She felt befouled, both by Elise's slime and the steps she had had to take to counteract its effect.

Mrs. Covey came softly into the silent room and looked compassionately at the pale girl who sat slumped on the edge of her desk, hands gripping and clenching around the edge in an involuntary spasm of disgust. She shut the door, separating the former combatants, and walked over to lay a comforting hand on Keri's shoulder.

Keri lifted a woeful face to the kindly one above her. "I feel sick, Mrs. Covey. I did what I had to, but I still feel sick. I've never had anyone hate me before, hate me so much that they wanted to hurt me." Keri shivered slightly.

"I think you need a cup of hot coffee," was Mrs. Covey's practical offer of sympathy. There was no blinking at the fact that Elise Barth was a spiteful, unpleasant bitch and nothing Mrs. Covey could say now would lessen the impact of the past harrowing minutes. She could only offer support and loyalty to the one who deserved it. She bustled out to the canteen and returned quickly with the steaming brew, well laced with sugar and cream. She noticed that Elise was still slumped over her desk, but there was no way she was going to offer coffee to that one!

Keri cradled the mug's warmth between her hands and sipped the heartening drink gratefully. "Thanks, Mrs. Covey. Thank you very much." There was more than gratitude for the coffee in those soft words. Keri was resilient and she was recovering swiftly. It would take

110

more than the Elise Barths of the world to send Keri to her knees.

Fortunately Keri's color was nearly back to normal when the closed door suddenly swung inward. Dain stood in the door, looking bewildered and a little helpless, much as many males are when confronted with an emotional woman.

"Er . . . ah . . . Miss Barth . . . That is, there seems to be something wrong with Miss Barth. I came into the office and she was . . . well, she looked ill, bent over her desk, but when I asked her what was wrong, she burst into tears and ran out of the office. Could one of you go after her and find out what's wrong?"

Keri and Mrs. Covey exchanged speaking looks. Mrs. Covey said, "Of course, Mr. Randolph, I'll go see what's wrong. Perhaps Miss Barth is ill. I understand that there's a twenty-four-hour flu going around."

"Oh, really?" Dain was basically uninterested in the state of Miss Barth's health except as it affected the smooth running of his office. "Well, if she's sick, send her home," he ordered a trifle impatiently. "Keri, I'll need you to take dictation." He turned and left abruptly, expecting Keri to follow immediately in his wake.

"Keri?" Mrs. Covey said softly. "The light dawns . . ." and she left the room in search of Elise, who by now was crying from chagrin and reaction in the women's rest room. Keri ground her teeth, gathered up her pad and pencils, and stormed out of the room in her turn.

By the time Mrs. Covey had dispatched a blotchy Miss Barth to the privacy and solace of her home, Keri had recorded four urgent letters at high speed and was typing them at Miss Barth's desk. She ripped them one by one from the typewriter, addressed the envelopes, and took

111

them back in to Dain for signature. He slashed a black scrawl across them and gathered up several files.

"Make sure those make the afternoon mail pickup. I'll be in conference with Simonds, Barkley, and Sturdevant. Don't disturb me unless the building collapses around your ears."

"Yes, Mr. Randolph," she acquiesced colorlessly, but her eyes spat icy green sparks. "I'll see that you're not disturbed, Mr. Randolph."

"I'll deal with you when I have more time, Keri," he promised dangerously, "but for now, here's something on account." Before she could evade him, he grasped her chin and lowered his mouth to hers.

Her mouth opened to object and he took full advantage of her instinctive gasp of outrage. His mouth closed over hers and ruthlessly plundered every sweet corner. The stroke of his tongue against hers was like no sensation she had ever experienced before. Their mouths became a fiery seal, welding them together for a timeless instant, lasting as long as infinity and as short as the beat of a heart. When Dain lifted his mouth from hers, Keri wasn't sure she'd ever be able to draw in breath again without recalling the taste of his lips.

He laid his free hand against the side of her neck and said softly, "If I had more time . . ." and left her standing there bemused, in the middle of his office, the carefully typed envelopes and letters in a scattered drift around her feet.

Finally she knelt carefully and gathered up her work. With trembling hands she laid them on his desk, and by concentrating solely on the task at hand, managed to fold the originals, stuff them into the proper envelopes, and reorder the file copies. The peppermint flavor of the first

112

envelope she licked clung to her suddenly dry tongue and she had to force moisture into her mouth to complete her task of sealing the envelopes and affixing the international airmail stamps. The Wright Brothers wore smug masculine smirks that she had never noticed before. She pounded them flat with a clenched fist, flattening the Kitty Hawk as well, for good measure. If she saw Dain Randolph's handsome, masculine face beneath her softly thumping fist, could she be blamed?

She went back out to Elise's desk, called down to the mail room for a pickup, and then looked in to see if Mrs. Covey was back from ministering to Elise. She found that good lady placidly continuing their work of the morning, entirely unperturbed by the day's tumultuous events.

"How . . . where is Elise?" Keri questioned hesitantly.

"She was sniveling in the rest room," Mrs. Covey replied succinctly. "By the way, call me Bridget, Keri, since we seem to be approaching a first-name basis in the office." She smiled cheerfully at a flushing Keri.

"Oh, Bridget," Keri said helplessly. "Don't you start on me too. Where is Elise now?"

"If she has any sense she'll be at home by now, but she may be perched on a bar stool somewhere for all I know. I put a cold, wet washcloth across her face to shut her up and then told her that Mr. Randolph thought perhaps she had the flu and felt she should go home and nurse it. If she's smart her flu will stretch out for a few days. I also," Bridget continued darkly, "reminded her not to forget those phone calls to her friends."

"You listened," Keri said faintly.

"The intercom was open between the rooms," Bridget admitted with airy unconcern. "You don't mess around, girl. You won't have any more trouble with Elise and she'll make those phone calls. She was a bully and you handled her just right. I listened because I thought you might need help, but I should have known better after I watched you take on the Thurston cat. That group of spiteful gossips will think three and four times before they start out to shred someone's reputation again. You didn't know it, but they've cheerfully wrecked several girls' reputations before this, so don't regret a single word of what you said. More power to your arm, I says."

Keri threw up her hands in surrender. "I give up, Bridget. I'm a public hero and I'll wear my laurels proudly."

"Heroine, my dear, heroine. Mr. Randolph expects precision from his highly paid executive secretaries."

"Mr. Randolph expects a hell of a lot from his secretaries," Keri muttered to herself, her face darkening. Bridget wisely didn't ask for a repeat of Keri's sotto voce comments.

"Are you manning, if you'll pardon the expression, Elise's desk, Keri? If so, I think someone just came in."

"I suppose so," Keri threw back over her shoulder as she went into the outer office to find the mail boy patiently waiting. His eyes widened appreciatively as Keri walked toward him, but he was wise enough to say nothing. Keri handed him the four envelopes with an admonition to be sure that they went out in the afternoon mail. He left, casting a surreptitious glance over his shoulder. He could now report with authority that Miss Dalton was a real smasher! If he were only ten years older and several thousand dollars richer . . .

The rest of the afternoon passed. That was all that could be said about it. Keri handled Miss Barth's regular duties and worked on her own as the opportunity arose. Bridget brought Keri another cup of coffee at mid-afternoon since

Keri felt at least one of them must remain in the office to answer the phone. There was also the unspoken but understood reason that Keri just wasn't up to enduring more speculative looks.

Keri had begun to pray that the rest of the day would pass on winged feet and that, most importantly, she would be gone before Dain returned from his conference. She had never been a clockwatcher before, but the agonizingly slow sweep of the minute hand as it crept toward five o'clock reminded her of the movie *The Day the Earth Stood Still*. The minute hand quivered and strained to bridge that last sixty-second gap between fifty-nine minutes and five o'clock. When it finally reached Keri's goal it seemed to shiver, exhausted, a runner who falls gasping through the tape at the end of the race.

Keri stuck her head into her old office. "Bridget, it's just gone five o'clock and I'm going home!" she announced in heartfelt tones.

"Go ye," Bridget adjured her. "Flee as though the 'deil' himself was after a-catching ye." She laughed at Keri's astounded expression. "My mother's granny was from the old land, but it doesn't need second sight to know that you'd rather not run up against Dain Randolph again today."

Keri glanced involuntarily around, as though the very mention of his name could be sufficient to conjure him up. Her grin was a bit forced, but then she and Bridget had gone through a lot together today. It was true that she wanted desperately to avoid Dain, but not exactly for the reasons Bridget thought. Bridget hadn't seen, nor been the recipient of, that traumatizing kiss. Keri didn't plan to be around when Dain had more time today.

Keri joined the departing stream of workers. There

were many appreciative glances, but no overtures. Rumor, supposition, and speculation swirled about her, cloaking her status in mystery, and so the aspiring Lotharios walked warily. No one wanted to be the one to try to poach on Dain Randolph's presumed territory.

Had Keri realized what lay behind her blessed isolation, she would have been upset, but she was so intent on escaping that nothing penetrated her abstraction. It's doubtful if she would have noticed any overture short of a forceable attempt at seduction! She was more attuned to the fear of hearing Dain's deep voice call her name or of feeling his powerful grip on her shoulder preventing her flight.

In spite of her morbid certainty that it couldn't possibly be as easy as this to get away from RanCo, Keri slipped into her car and gunned it from the parking lot without hail or hindrance. Fortunately for Keri, sometimes there isn't a policeman around when you don't want him, because she darted through the evening traffic like a rabbit running broken field for its burrow. If there happened to be an opening, she took it. If an opening wasn't available, she made one. From the new Randolph Building at Tyson's Corner, Virginia, where RanCo was housed, to her apartment in Alexandria, Keri ducked and wove her agile way through the homeward-bound traffic. She parked her car and sprinted to the waiting elevator. If Schyler had been unlucky enough to have been lurking to waylay her, she would have left footprints on his chest in her haste to reach her apartment.

She slid the key into the lock, turned the doorknob in one smooth motion, and pulled the door open. She entered the apartment, shot the deadbolt, and kicked off her shoes in practically simultaneous motions. Her purse and keys went on the nearest table, her jacket caught momentarily

116

on the arm of the overstuffed chair and then slid to the floor in an untidy heap. Keri didn't even pause. If ever anyone deserved a drink, she did.

A survey of the contents of her refrigerator was disappointing. There was no chilled white wine, her preferred drink, so she dropped a few ice cubes into a six-ounce tumbler, splashed in a large dollop of Amaretto, and filled the rest of the glass with club soda. The soda cut the richness of the Amaretto and the sweet bite of the liqueur was velvet smooth over her tongue.

She stood in the middle of her small kitchen, contemplating the glass she rolled reflectively between her palms. For dinner she had left a small steak marinating all day in a gin and ginger teriyaki sauce. She had put it on the counter when she came in to warm to room temperature. The broiled steak, sided by saffron rice and a tossed green salad, heavy on the cherry tomatoes and cucumbers, would suffice. Should she eat or bathe first?

A warm, relaxing bubble-filled bath . . . her old family doctor couldn't have written a better prescription. Keri sipped delicately at the drink she had carried into the bathroom with her. She lifted a slender leg and watched the bubbles run from her ankle, over the curve of her calf to the back of her knee to rejoin the high drift of scented bubbles around her thighs.

Deep in the heated peace of the water her tension-taut muscles had at last started to unknot and she found she could consider the day's events with some measure of detachment.

Miss Barth. That viper's fangs had been pulled. Keri had the leverage now and she'd not hesitate to use it. Miss Barth had woefully underestimated her opponent and the price she'd have to pay for that miscalculation would be a civil tongue and a fair division of labor. Dain Randolph might not notice it, but his office was going to be a happier place to work, for at least two of his secretaries.

In the short time she had been one of Dain's secretaries, pre-transformation Keri had pegged Elise as a typical office tyrant. Bridget had been doing more than her fair division of the office output for a long time. Like many of her kind, the glamorous Elise had shirked hard work when she could shift it over to another desk. Elise had answered phones prettily and taken dictation crisply, but it had been Bridget and later Keri who turned out most of the flawlessly typed letters for Dain's signature. Well, from now on Elise's nails would lose their feline length and get clipped to accommodate the typing she was going to have to do! The thought gave Keri no end of satisfaction.

The water was cooling and the bubbles dissolving rapidly in a spatter of tiny pops. Keri felt clean, languid, and slightly hollow. She flipped the drain lever up with her toe, stood up, pulled the shower curtain closed, and rinsed off with a quick warm shower spray. She patted dry with a thick terry towel, smoothed on Chantilly body lotion with long deft strokes, and finished with a scented dusting of the matching powder.

The diluted dregs of her drink went down the washbasin as she pulled out the pins that secured her high-piled hair. It tumbled down in a tousled mass to frame a face that still showed the effects of the emotional day. Keri's green eyes had a harassed and haunted air and she noticed that, in repose, her mouth was still firmly pulled in at the edges.

Keri slipped into fresh bikini briefs and a thin, peasant-style long housedress. The off-the-shoulder style didn't allow for a bra, but she wasn't going anywhere. It was a comfortable dress, and the abstract swirl of blues and greens with touches of rust falling in a long sweep to the floor from the elastic band under her breasts, was a cheerful splash of color, suitable for lightening a black mood.

The meal helped her hollow feeling, but didn't really seem to do much for her mental condition. She still had slightly sick twinges whenever she thought about the day's events, and after she had washed and put away the dinner dishes she fixed herself an Irish coffee and curled up on her couch. Mendelssohn and Mozart held no appeal for her this evening so she hunted through her collection and located some Mireille Mathieu records. The clear, rich, sometimes sad, sometimes happy tones of the French singer seemed to fit her mood perfectly.

She was relaxed on the couch, happily, at last, thinking of nothing in particular when, in the middle of "Ciao, Mon Coeur," the doorbell began its irritating and totally unwelcome announcement. Keri shot up off the couch in a reflex action and stood, heart pounding, trying to regain the composure that the abrupt, unexpected summons had destroyed.

"Oh, blast! And the peephole hasn't been installed yet," she wailed to herself. She tried to ignore the repeated chiming, but whoever was on the other side of her front door knew she was in there and wasn't going to go away. "If that's Schyler I'll have his guts for garters, as Granny used to say," she muttered as she stalked up to the door.

As soon as she began to manipulate the deadbolt, the doorbell fell silent. Keri hissed in exasperation as the lock hung momentarily and then released. She pulled the door back and stood uncompromisingly in the doorway, barring entrance to her apartment. If she'd had a flaming sword handy she would have waved it for effect. She wasn't in the mood for company!

CHAPTER 6

Dain towered over her and, from the look of him, wasn't in any better mood than she was. He was still dressed as he had been at the office except that he had removed his tie and stuffed it into the pocket of his jacket, which he carried slung over his shoulder.

"You shouldn't just open the door, Keri," he growled. "You don't know who might be on the other side. Get your landlord to install a peephole."

"You're absolutely right! Go away!" Keri spoke through clenched teeth. She started to step back into her apartment but stopped when he took a step after her. Obviously he planned to follow her inside. She blocked the doorway. "What do you want?" she asked in her most inhospitable voice. "You can't come in."

"I want to talk to you and I can come in." As he spoke he draped his coat over the doorknob of her door, and grasping her firmly about the waist, lifted her in one smooth motion back into the apartment, setting her to one side of the door. He retrieved his coat from the doorknob, shut the door behind him, and much as Keri had done when she came into the apartment earlier, tossed his coat at the nearest chair. His aim was better than hers had been.

It wouldn't do any good to sputter "You can't do this" to Dain, because he *had* done it, but Keri wasn't ready to accept a heavy-handed fait accompli. She planted her hands on her hips and regarded him wrathfully. "I don't want to talk to you, Dain Randolph. I've had my fill of RanCo today, and that includes its major stockholder. Go home!"

He ignored her. He glanced around the comfortable room and cocked an ear at the music. "Very nice." He seemed to be including and approving both her decorating and musical tastes in that succinct appraisal. Keri seethed.

Before she could say anything though, Dain rubbed the back of his neck wearily and announced abruptly, "I'm hungry. Can you fix me something? I just got out of the meeting with Simonds and the others. We didn't stop to eat and I'm starved. I came directly here," he added unnecessarily.

Since she obviously wasn't going to be able to shift him bodily, she decided that perhaps if she fed him and gave him a drink he might go peacefully. It had worked with Schyler, even though he had brought his own provisions, she amended with an inner, mental smile. Besides, Dain had said he wanted to talk to her and she knew him well enough by now to know that he wouldn't go until he had said all he planned to.

"All right, I'll feed you," she agreed with less than complete enthusiasm. "Come fix yourself a drink and then stay out of my kitchen. Today's *Washington Post* is on the coffee table and you can choose whatever type of music you're in the mood for."

"Yes, ma'am," he responded with suspicious meekness and followed her obediently into the small kitchen. While she started the meal preparations he poured himself a hefty scotch and then removed his bulk from the kitchen with lamblike docility. Soon Grieg's Piano Concerto in A Minor filtered into the kitchen. Now *what* kind of mood did that indicate?

Keri took a sizable T-bone steak out of the freezer, sprinkled it heavily with a special herbed and seasoned salt and ran it under the broiler. He looked like a medium-rare-steak eater. In her lower oven she reheated the saffron rice she'd cooked for her own supper, plus a couple of brown-and-serve rolls. She tossed another green salad, threw on cherry tomatoes and sliced cucumber with a heavy hand, and dosed the whole salad with Parmesan cheese and Italian dressing. The steak was ready to turn, so she seasoned the other side and began to set the small dining table. By the time she'd laid the table, carried in the salad, and dished up the rice and rolls, the steak was ready. She slapped the steak on the plate beside the rice, grabbed up the butter dish and marched back to the dining alcove.

"Do you want water, coffee, tea, or another drink with your meal?" She spoke to indicate that she was ready for him to come to the table. He hadn't been reading the proffered newspaper. He'd been stretched out on her couch, shoes off, hands clasped behind his head, staring up at the ceiling.

When she spoke, he turned his head lazily and then sat up with complete aplomb. He slipped back into his shoes, skirted the coffee table, bending to pick up his now empty glass as he passed by, and approached the table. She watched his eyes widen when he saw what she'd managed to arrange for his delectation and he grinned ruefully at her, with just a touch of apology.

"I didn't mean for you to go to a lot of trouble. I expected something on the order of a cheese sandwich or an omelet. This is a feast." The look he cast over the succulent steak was frankly rapacious.

"I make lousy omelets," she informed him, grinning slightly, "and you looked hungry."

"I am," he agreed smoothly, but he wasn't looking at the steak anymore.

"Sit, eat," she urged. For a moment he had looked as though food were the furthest thing from his mind, and she wanted his attention firmly fixed on the steak, not on her face and mouth! She had the sinking feeling that Dain wasn't going to be as easily gotten rid of as Schyler had been.

The steak won, for the moment at least, but Keri had no idea by how narrow a margin. While Dain began to eat, Keri fixed him some instant iced tea at his request and then came to sit across from him at the table. She had fixed herself another very weak Amaretto and soda and she sipped on it from time to time as she watched him dispose entirely of the meal.

When he had eaten the last morsel of the last roll, he got up and carried his dishes and silverware into the kitchen. He hadn't spoken another word while he was eating, which was fine with Keri because her fund of small talk had dried up and blown away. Dain didn't look as forbidding as he had when he came in the door but he couldn't by any stretch of the imagination be called relaxed and expansive either. There was something on his mind and

Keri was afraid that she was soon going to find out just what it was! She was also pretty sure that she was going to wish that she *hadn't* found out by the time he got finished!

"Just leave the dishes, Dain. I'll do them with the breakfast dishes in the morning," Keri called into the kitchen. She really planned to do them as soon as he was gone, but she didn't fancy a cozy domestic scene where she washed and he dried in the close confines of her small kitchen. The nearer Dain got, the more dangerous he was to her peace of mind. She could still taste that kiss he had given her in his office.

Dain appeared in the kitchen door. "I am reasonably domesticated," he offered mildly, but there was a glint in his eye she disliked exceedingly. It was the same look the spider might have worn when he said the oft-quoted lines, "Come into my parlor . . ."

She shook her head decisively, and said, "No, Dain." She put a lot of feeling and emphasis into that no, but when Dain smiled she knew that even if he had gotten the deeper message he wasn't going to be a man who took no for an answer.

He walked toward her. She sat rigidly in her chair, her eyes fixed on his. He didn't stop until he was directly in front of her, which meant her neck was stretched upward at an uncomfortable angle, but she couldn't seem to wrest her gaze away from his. His hand came slowly up from his side, almost unwillingly, and he ran the tips of his fingers lightly but firmly from the angle of her jaw beneath her left ear down the taut line of her neck to her shoulder.

Time's progress and her ability to breathe seemed to have ceased. His hand slid slowly, carefully, around to the back of her neck, beneath the heavy weight of her hair, and exerted a gentle but remorseless pull to bring her to her feet. When she was standing, no more than inches separated the lengths of their bodies from full and intimate contact. She could feel his nearness with the invisible sensors of her whole skin, but she could see only the compelling green of his eyes, could trace the starlike paths of lighter color raying out from the dark wells of his pupils.

"I have time now, Keri," he said deeply, his voice rising in a husky rumble from the depths of the broad chest she somehow, naturally and inescapably, swayed against.

I shouldn't . . . I can't . . . she thought incoherently, but she was going to.

He had time, and he took it. This was a kiss of infinite duration, slow, seductive, and thorough. The taste of his mouth was excitingly familiar as was the soft rasp of his tongue against her own in a duel of exploration.

Keri felt all her resolutions buckle, as well as her knees, but it didn't seem to matter because Dain was supporting her, his arms a living, heated bar around her waist and shoulders. When his mouth finally, reluctantly, left her own and time took up a march in tune to the heavy race of her heartbeat, Keri could only sag weakly against the support of his hard body.

"I didn't mean to do that," Dain murmured softly into her hair. Keri had been concentrating on the heavy throb of the heart pulsing in the chest next to her ear, but the sound wasn't loud enough to drown out those rueful words. Her knees stiffened and so did her spine and her arms. She shoved against him, hard. He staggered back a step or two—she didn't accomplish much because he took her with him.

Since brute force hadn't worked, she tried words next. "Since you wish you hadn't done it, perhaps you'll be good

126

enough to release me now," she requested in her most quelling tones.

"I didn't say I wished I hadn't done it," he corrected her mildly. "I said I hadn't meant to do it." He released her and smiled a tiger's smile. "At least not just yet. I want to talk to you." The smile died away and an echo of the grim expression he had been wearing when she opened the door to her apartment firmed the lines of his face. He looked stern and determined and in no mood for argument.

She was still tempted to give him one. After all, this was her apartment and she'd fed him and been perfectly civil . . . well, perhaps not *perfectly* civil, but still . . . It was just prolonging the inevitable, she recognized. He wouldn't go until he'd had his say and she was suddenly very tired.

"All right, Dain. Say what you must, and then go. It's been a long, tiring day." She was afraid to add the concomitant *and I'd like to go to bed.* He had shown himself distractible and she didn't plan to distract him right into her bedroom!

They sat down on the couch and Keri tucked her feet up beneath the full skirt of her dress. Dain didn't try to crowd her—he sat a cushion's width away—but his arm lay along the back of the couch, his hand just a touch away from her shoulder. She was uncomfortably conscious of the nearness of that hand.

"You said you'd had a long day," he said obliquely. "Would you like to tell me what made it longer than usual? When I came back to the office to collect some files and you at five past five, you were gone. I had to draft Mrs. Covey to take notes and her shorthand is *slow.* Are you going to turn into a clockwatcher?"

Keri was cautious. His words were superficially jesting,

but the tone was probing and serious. She said carefully, "My normal hours are from 8:30 to 5:00. I hadn't been notified that you would want me to work overtime tonight."

Dain dropped the indirect approach. "Elise Barth will get her notice tomorrow." Keri risked a sideways glance at Dain. He wasn't looking at her just then, but rather staring across the room into space. His face was set in savage lines.

"You . . . you've heard something," Keri forced through dry lips.

"Heard something? Heard something! I've heard sly snickers and veiled innuendos and Barkley even jabbed me in the ribs with his elbow."

Keri nearly laughed at this ultimate outrage, but it really wasn't funny. Dain was furious and the situation could prove explosive. She wasn't sure just how to defuse it, but she had to try.

"How did you connect Elise with . . ." She gestured expressively, unable to put the whole wretched situation into words.

"It wasn't hard," he replied grimly. "I'm not blind, you know. I knew she fancied me, but I didn't fancy her." Keri sucked in breath at this masculine arrogance and gave Dain a look of pure dislike. It was wasted because he wasn't looking at her. "I knew she wasn't going to take kindly to your . . . ah . . . transformation, but I thought she'd have more sense of self-preservation." He looked at her directly. "And don't quote the old saw about the woman scorned. I never gave her the slightest encouragement. All that I asked of her was that she be a competent secretary and keep her personal feelings to herself. What

I do in my private life is no concern of hers. She meddled and she hurt you, so she has to go."

"But how did you hear?" Keri pursued.

"Barkley's secretary is evidently a crony of Miss Barth's and she passed on some choice tidbits of fallacious reasoning brewed up by my ex-secretary. Barkley was in turn merely congratulating me on my good fortune." Dain's voice was heavy with irony.

Keri wasn't listening to the irony. She was nearly beside herself with rage. She hated Dain and she hated Mr. Barkley and she hated the whole smug masculine assumption that, were she attractive enough, a secretary cum mistress could be considered one of the perks of an executive's job! At least Schyler had offered her marriage!

It nearly choked her, but she knew what she had to say. "You aren't going to fire Elise. If you fire her you'll only add fuel to the speculation. If everything remains the same, the gossip will die away quickly and I've already taken steps to make sure it'll go no further."

It would be too much to expect that he would just accept her word on the matter and not pursue it further. After all, *she* was the injured party. Dain had started to object when a thought seemed to occur to him.

"What steps?" he questioned with evidence of great interest.

Keri wasn't going to repeat any of those conversations verbatim. "Never mind," she said hastily. "I spoke to Elise and one of her friends. I can assure you that the story will go no further and Elise will do all in her power to repair the damage. If you fire her, you'll lend veracity to her gossip, so just leave it alone. I promise that Elise's claws have been cut."

A belated thought struck Dain. "Elise doesn't have the

129

flu, does she?" He pursed his lips in a silent whistle. "You must have gotten finished with her just before I came in. She looked wiped out." He came to a decision. "I think you're right. You won't have any more trouble with her. D'you want to take over her job and put her in with Mrs. Covey? I'd like to have you in the outer office."

Keri stared at him in disbelief. He was offering her a choice instead of merely saying "Thus it shall be." Elise's collapse must really have impressed him. It didn't make any difference. She didn't want to be in the outer office, whatever Dain might want. Elise was welcome to be front woman.

For the duration of her stay, and the probable duration grew shorter with each passing day, Keri was determined to maintain a low profile. Keri was going to have another talk with Charles in the near future. With his contacts in the State Department she could have her choice of embassies or legations anywhere in the world, and any part of the world except the Washington, D.C., area looked mighty good to her tonight. And she wouldn't go as a secretary. She'd arrange to take her Foreign Service rating exams and once she left RanCo, she'd make sure she was on the other side of the desk from now on! It had taken a long time for the lesson to sink in, but it was well rooted at last.

Dain was waiting for her answer. "No, thank you," Keri declined politely. "I don't think it would be a good idea to make any changes in the office hierarchy at this point."

He snorted. "So you prefer to run my office from behind the scenes, do you? Well, all right. Just keep Elise in line. It won't be for too long anyway."

She looked at him suspiciously, but his face was now

relaxed and bland. She hugged her own secret plans and agreed. "No, it won't be for long." Let him read what he would into that simple statement.

He didn't seem to like what he read. With a decisive movement he came closer to her on the couch, catching the back of her neck in a gentle but inexorable grip to prevent her escape. His fingers again wove their way into her thick hair and gently pulled, tilting her face up so that she was forced to look directly at him.

"Somehow," he mused, "I don't think we mean the same thing when we say, 'It won't be for long.' You wouldn't be planning to seek other employment in the near future, would you? And perhaps disappear from the area, leaving no forwarding address, hmm, my sweet?"

Keri tried to keep a look of blank incomprehension pasted over her face, but she didn't think she was succeeding. She was feeling the magnetic pull of Dain's attraction too strongly. She wished he'd go home!

"You seem to have a habit of skipping out, Keri, darling," he stated insistently and persuasively. "You wouldn't be thinking of becoming some other man's secretary, now would you?"

His fingers were now stroking firmly up and down the back of her neck. It should have relaxed the tense muscles back there, but the touch of his hard fingers was having the opposite effect. She had to brace herself against responding to the warm seduction of his expert massage. "No, Dain, I don't plan to become another man's secretary," she managed to say in slightly breathless tones.

"Now why don't I feel satisfied with that answer?" he spoke his thoughts aloud. "I think because it leaves so much unpromised, Keri," he concluded. "You wouldn't

131

care to expand on the scope of your promise, would you?" It was practically a royal command.

Keri braced herself. "No." She refused bluntly. She hated to give so much away, but she wouldn't lie to him, nor would she make any promises she didn't intend to keep.

"Ah-ha." He didn't seem surprised. "Charles, I presume. Have you spoken to him yet? Or hasn't there been time?" Still that hand stroked gently up and down her neck.

"There hasn't been time," she admitted grudgingly. She wanted to tell him it was time for him to go home, but she didn't quite dare. A strange tension was rising between them, coiling and tightening with each exchange of words. She was afraid that one wrong word would spark a reaction from Dain which she couldn't, or wouldn't, handle.

"Any particular country in mind or are you just going to take pot luck?" Now there was a sharp bite to his question and the hand had stopped stroking gently. His hand moved down across the top line of her shoulder, exploring the bare expanse of skin before it journeyed to clasp the point of her shoulder.

Suddenly she realized that he was sitting right next to her, his thigh pressed warmly (and warningly?) against her own. She wasn't exactly sure how this had come about —she hadn't noticed his further encroachment—but here he definitely was.

"I haven't got any country in mind," she protested a bit feebly. "I just thought that . . ."

She wasn't allowed to get another word out. "Don't think, Keri," Dain ordered. "It'll just get you into trouble." And his mouth swooped down to close off further words and thought.

132

When she surfaced for the first time it was to the realization that his kisses became even more devastating with increased exposure. Familiarity bred a desire for more familiarity. She sank beneath the onslaught of his expert seduction for a second time.

He never gave her a chance to think, to protest. Each deep, probing kiss sapped her will to resist further. His tongue touched and tasted, sipping the nectar of her mouth like a honeybee dipping into a fragrant flower. He sucked her lower lip gently into his mouth and caressed the pouted fullness with a gentle, questing tongue tip. The corners of her mouth, the line of her upper lip, all were traced and teased until her mouth was softly swollen, aching for his further possession.

When he lifted her, positioning her across his lap, Keri merely looped an arm behind his back and sank again down the ladder into the deep well of passion, for the third time, without a murmur of complaint. As he whispered, "Oh, God, you're beautiful, Keri, darling," she stroked the hard line of his jaw, enjoying the beginnings of his beard, a texture which didn't scrape, but felt excitingly masculine.

She wondered . . . and then she felt the drag, sensuously rough, of his cheek across the tender skin of her breasts. She was supported by his left arm, stretched out across his lap, and his right hand had been stroking the warm skin of her throat. With an unhurried motion he stroked down beneath the loose top to cup her breasts, and his mouth followed in hungry pursuit to capture the pink-brown crest of the ripe mound his fingers so lovingly molded. The drawing pressure of his lips sent an electric tingle shooting down into the pit of her stomach where it arced and flared into a deep, burning holocaust. He started to slide the sleeve of the dress down her arm.

She whimpered, a sound of mindless acquiescence. She was his for the taking . . . and the phone began to ring. "Leave it," he whispered, lifting his head slightly and then returning to his preoccupation. She tried, but the insistent summons began to pull her up, rung by painful rung, back into the air of sanity. The waters of passion receded slowly, but he could feel the altering character of her response.

Keri struggled to surface. "Dain, the phone. I must . . ." She sat up dizzily, and he sighed. With reluctant fingers he helped her adjust her dress and boosted her up off his lap.

"Next month don't pay your phone bill," he ordered her half fiercely.

Keri walked unsteadily to the kitchen and lifted the receiver. She held it to her ear and said, "Hello?" in a husky croak. Her throat didn't seem to be working properly.

She turned back to look at Dain, a bewildered expression on her face. "There wasn't anyone there. They hung up." She held the receiver in her hand as though not quite sure what to do next. Her mental processes were laborious, still hazed by her deep submersion in passion. She shook her head slightly, as though to clear it.

"Hang up the phone, Keri," he ordered softly. "Come back here to me."

Keri's brain was clearing fast. She hung up the phone, but she didn't go back into Dain's waiting arms. She wasn't sure of much right then, but the one thing she did know was that if she got within five feet of him she was lost. Now that sanity was returning she wasn't sure that she wanted to be lost. She might never find her way again.

"Come here, darling," he repeated softly. She was so lovely, the soft folds of her long gown swirling gracefully down to the floor and her eyes huge and still drowsy with the lingering remnants of desire. The scent of her perfumed skin still drifted around him, but it was poor substitute for the satin warmth of her body.

"No, Dain. No and no." Her voice was stronger. She was regaining control rapidly. "I shouldn't have . . . we shouldn't have. . . . I won't come back. And you stay right where you are!" But he showed signs of coming to her instead.

He sank back on the couch, a rueful smile creasing the corners of his mouth. "All right, Keri. Remind me to sell my AT&T stock tomorrow."

She grinned slightly at this sally and managed to retort, "Really? I planned to buy more. Marvelous invention, the telephone. I wouldn't be without one."

"Point taken, Keri." He looked very serious and said quietly, "Don't call Charles for a while, Keri. Promise me that you'll wait and that you'll talk to me before you start pulling strings. Give me a little time."

"Time for what, Dain?" *Time to complete what you just started?* she questioned herself silently.

"Time for you to learn to trust me, Keri. You don't now, do you?"

He still lounged at ease on the couch, across the room from her, but the tension was starting to build between them again. She could feel the caress of his eyes and she knew that if she didn't get him out of her apartment right now, she would soon have good reason not to trust him.

"No, I don't trust you, Dain," she admitted candidly. "But may it comfort you to know that, after this episode,

135

I don't trust myself either." There was no reason not to admit it, because she truly couldn't deny her willing participation in the events of the past minutes. She certainly hadn't struggled wildly for her virtue!

"And now, if I'm to learn to trust you, I suggest that it's time for you to go."

"Have I your promise?" he insisted as he rose obediently to his feet.

"I don't know, Dain," she replied in a troubled voice. "If I give it, it will only be a conditional promise at best. I can't promise not to talk to Charles, but I will promise not to do so just on the basis of whatever gossip is currently being circulated about us."

"So I'm to be put on my best behavior," he said grimly.

"If you want to call it that," she agreed stiffly. "I prefer to see it as a desire not to see the situation at work exacerbated further."

"Damn it, Keri, it's *my* company!"

"Damn it, Dain, it's *my* reputation!" She continued. "You may own the company, but you don't own the employees' tongues, nor can you control them. It isn't practical to fire everyone who gossips about us. I prefer to give them nothing damaging to gossip about."

"I refuse categorically to call you Miss Dalton at work," he protested, but she knew she'd won.

"I shall call you Mr. Randolph, however," she said firmly.

"All right, Keri. In the office. But I'll make the rules out of the office," he promised darkly.

"You can try," she said demurely and then grinned wickedly. "Go on home, Dain, and let me get some rest."

He gathered up his coat and said formally, "Thank you for the meal, Keri. It was delicious . . . all of it."

136

She blushed, delightfully he thought, and opened the front door. "Out, Dain!" He stopped before her and tipped up her chin with a long forefinger. "I'll see you tomorrow, Keri." He kissed her lips gently, making no demands.

"I don't suppose you'd like to go back abroad and buy another company, would you?" she asked a trifle wistfully.

"Certainly," he agreed promptly. "When can we leave? I'll even let you pick the company and the country. I've never bothered to travel with a secretary before. I can tell it would be a great convenience . . . dictation taken at all hours of the day and night."

She threw up her hands in despair and shoved him out the door. She heard his chuckle as she closed it firmly behind him and locked the deadbolt. He was finally locked out of her apartment but he wasn't easily banished from her thoughts, and, she suspected ruefully, from her dreams.

Keri cleaned the kitchen for the second time and as she was drying her hands, the phone rang again. This time she got to it by the second ring.

"Hello?"

"Where have you been? I called earlier."

"None of your business, Schyler. I'm not accountable to you." She was short with him, but not as short as she might have been because she owed him. How delicious to know that it had been a call from Schyler that saved her from Dain.

"I've been in New York, but I'm back now. I want you to go out with me this weekend. I have tickets for the Kennedy Center for Saturday night, and we'll have dinner at the Tavern in Georgetown." He sounded supremely confident.

"I shall send you a hearing aid because you are obviously hard of hearing. I am not going anywhere, anytime with you, Schyler." She nearly screamed into the phone.

"I'll pick you up at seven thirty, Keri," he said, ignoring her angry exclamation completely. "Good night, my darling." He hung up.

Keri threw the phone receiver back into its rest. "I hate men! All men, in every shape, size and form. I . . . hate . . . men!" That outburst did little to relieve her feelings. She flounced off to bed.

The next morning she went to work spoiling for a fight. She couldn't find any opponents, however. Elise was still out with "flu" and Dain called in to say that he would be away from the office until mid-afternoon. Since Bridget Covey declined the honor of manning the outer office, it fell to Keri, little as she desired it.

The morning passed quietly and Keri calmed somewhat. She no longer desired the head of *any* man who crossed her path, served up on a plate. She would be content with just Schyler's, well garnished with parsley. Talk about people who couldn't take a hint . . . Schyler wouldn't know a hint if it blew up in his face.

When the door to the outer corridor opened, Keri looked up from her typing with a politely welcoming smile smoothed on her face. The woman who confronted her didn't return the smile. She regarded Keri much as she might have regarded a large horsefly swimming in her borscht. With disgust.

Keri's smile faded. She was tempted to glance behind herself to see if perhaps the woman was looking at someone else. No one had ever looked at Keri with that expression. Keri didn't like it.

The woman was beautiful. Keri had to admit it. She was also beautifully and expensively dressed. Her hair obvi-

138

ously had the benefit of the services of the finest beauticians, because what Keri judged to be the normal warm brown color had been artfully tipped and highlighted, dramatizing what would otherwise be a pleasant but not exciting hue. Her eyes were hazel and hard. She exuded wealth, assurance, and arrogance. That gave Keri a clue to her identity.

"May I help you?" Keri questioned politely.

"I doubt it," was the totally uncivil reply.

Keri was nonplussed. Active hostility radiated from the woman and Keri was at a loss to understand why. To the best of her knowledge she had never seen . . . no, that wasn't strictly accurate, Keri realized. She had glimpsed this woman before, but where? Ah-ha, she had it!

The woman had been with the group of people who had walked past her at the time she had seen Schyler again for the first time in six months. He had been part of that group, had, in fact, been at the side of the woman who now faced her. Keri had noticed her in passing only, but her memory for faces was excellent. She was also afraid she could put a name to the face.

"I'm Denise Randolph. I've come to have lunch with my brother." The tone said, I don't have to explain a thing to you, peasant.

Denise started to sweep grandly past Keri. Keri said quietly, "I'm sorry, Miss Randolph, but your brother isn't in his office. He hasn't come in at all this morning. Was he expecting you?"

"I don't have to make appointments with my brother, Miss Dalton," Denise sneered. "Where is he?"

Keri wondered how Denise Randolph knew her name. Surely Dain hadn't discussed her with his sister. And from what Bridget had said when describing the less than

139

charming manner Lady Denise displayed toward her brother's wage slaves, Denise wasn't the type to go out of her way to learn the names of salaried workers just to make a good impression. She certainly wasn't trying to make a good impression on Keri right now.

"Mr. Randolph called a while ago to say he was lunching in D.C. with Señor Villarreal. I believe he plans to return to the office by mid-afternoon." Keri's voice was smoothly neutral.

"Where are they lunching?" Denise snapped.

"I'm sorry, Miss Randolph, Mr. Randolph didn't say."

"Would you like to leave a message?" Keri called softly to Denise's retreating back. "I guess there was no message," Keri answered herself as the door slammed behind Denise.

"Did I hear the dulcet tones of la belle Denise?" Bridget inquired, coming into Keri's office.

"You certainly did," Keri grinned. She shook her hand, as one might when one's fingers have encountered hot metal. "Madame was not pleased. Brother not available to pick up tab for lunch. Madame departed in high dudgeon."

"A not unusual condition for Madame," Bridget asserted dryly. "The only time she's civil is when Brother is with her, or if she's accompanied by some other male she's trying to impress. I've never seen her with a female friend."

"I'm sure she has many," Keri asserted piously. "They just won't be found working for a living." She wasn't generally catty, but Denise's attitude, added to Keri's previous problems, rankled unwontedly, causing normally buried feline instincts to surface. She made a face at Bridget, "Miau, pfft, pfft."

140

Bridget laughed. "Are you ready for lunch, Keri?"

"Ravenous. Infighting always gives me an appetite. Are we eating in or out today?"

"I'll leave that up to you," Bridget said cautiously.

"Oh, in, I think. I might as well see how well yesterday's intervention has worked. If there's too much headturning and subdued whispering, I might have to call Elise. Besides it's never good strategy to procrastinate when faced with a painful necessity. As Dryden said: 'All delays are dangerous in war.' "

Keri notified the switchboard to handle all calls to Dain's office, then she and Bridget sallied forth.

All things considered, it wasn't too bad. There were some whispered conferences, to be sure, but well within the range of what Keri considered normal. She also took careful note of the attitude of the various men they encountered. There was admiration but very little salacious speculation that she could detect. Had she been irrevocably branded as Dain's mistress, Keri knew that her reception would have been considerably different. Most men in the cafeteria would have looked at her with a certain knowledge, the knowledge that she had her price and, for the present, Dain was paying it. They would have been wondering if they, too, could afford her price when Dain had ceased to pay.

CHAPTER 7

Dain strode into the outer office at two thirty. An eyebrow quirked when he saw Keri composedly typing at Elise's desk, but he didn't comment on Elise's continued absence. "Come into my office, Keri," he ordered as he headed toward the door to his own office.

"Of course, Mr. Randolph," Keri agreed meekly. Dain glared at her, but Keri managed to keep a straight face even though her eyes danced merrily. "Oh, by the way, Mr. Randolph, your sister came to the office this morning."

A strange expression, almost apprehensive, flitted across his face. "What the devil did Denise say to you?" he barked.

"Why . . . why nothing," Keri stammered, disconcerted by his reaction. "She expected you to take her to lunch. She wasn't . . . ah . . . pleased to discover you weren't here," Keri explained carefully. "She left immediately."

"Oh, that's all right then. I'll call her later." He was so

obviously relieved that Keri wondered. "Come on in, Keri." He stood in the doorway, waiting for her.

Fortunately the phone rang just at that moment, to Keri's relief. She signed that she'd follow after handling the call and he had to be content with that. He went into the office and Keri felt like wiping a metaphorical hand across a sweaty brow. She needed a moment to restore her equilibrium and her pulse rate.

She had always been aware of the virile attraction Dain possessed in such abundant measure, starting from the moment she had walked into his office that first day. It had, however, been a wary awareness because of her previous experiences and her firm resolve to avoid all office entanglements.

Dain had been equally resolved not to allow her to remain aloof. He had moved swiftly to pry her out of her protective shell, and having once wrenched her from her safe chrysalis, he had forced her to acknowledge, by her response to his kisses and caresses, that she was by no means indifferent to him. Keri was sure that he wasn't going to be content to stop at that point.

Schyler had been no real threat, posing nothing more than nuisance value, though he would have been appalled to hear himself so described. Her initial mild interest—he had been a pleasurable escort until he got out of hand— had changed rapidly to intense irritation when he continued to press his suit. Dain was an entirely different proposition.

Keri wasn't sure what he was proposing to begin with, and what was worse, she wasn't at all confident of her ability to refuse him, *whatever* he proposed. Last night had been an eye-opener for Keri, in more ways than one. She had to admit that she had heretofore overestimated her self-control. She now knew that Dain could melt the walls of her defenses like sea water running over the walls of a sand castle at the beach.

The light flashed angrily, summoning her into the inner sanctum. Dain was getting impatient. Keri stood up, smoothed her blue linen dress down nervously, grabbed up pad and pencils to give her something to do with her hands (she didn't really believe Dain wanted to see her for the purpose of giving her dictation) and went in to beard the lion in his lair. She didn't think she was going to make a very good Daniel and be able to escape unscathed from the den.

"About time," Dain grumbled when she came in. "Close the door behind you, Keri," he added when she left it ajar.

She retraced her steps and obediently closed it. When she turned, she bumped her nose into his chest. He had approached cat-footed behind her and she turned right into his arms. She didn't even have time for a scandalized wail of "Dain!" before his mouth swooped to cover hers.

She tried to keep her lips firmly closed against the insidious invasion, but Dain was relentless. He wanted surrender and he got it. He ran the tip of his tongue over the surface of her lips, gently probing through to the locked gate of her teeth. There was nothing rough or harsh about his wooing, just that insistent, persuasive tongue tip, touching, tantalizing, seeking entry to give and take pleasure. Keri made a sound deep in her throat and abandoned her resistance. She really didn't want to fight Dain anyway.

Somehow, during her surrender, her arms crept up around his neck while Dain swiveled to lean back against the door. This pulled Keri forward, forcing her to press fully against his body, and she was supported almost totally by his long legs and torso. In this intimate position it was immediately apparent that Dain was deeply affected by her ardent response and Keri hazily realized that if one of them didn't call a halt soon, whoever came through that door next was going to get the shock of his or her life.

I'll do it in a minute, she thought fuzzily. *Just one minute more.* When Keri's resistance to Dain collapsed, it did so most thoroughly.

Dain's hands came up to frame her face, the palms lying warmly at the angles of her jaw, the fingers threading over and behind her ears. He moved her face gently back and forth, sweeping his lips from side to side across her tender mouth.

Keri's own hands were busy, weaving in and out of the thick, silky hair at the back of his head. Her palms shaped to the hard bones of his skull, instinctively compressing and releasing in an age-old rhythm.

Dain's bête noire, the telephone, remained silent for once, but gradually the realization that this was neither the time nor the place was borne in upon them both. Dain brought them gently down from a plateau of frenzy, holding Keri close against his body and dropping little soothing kisses over her cheeks, eyelids, and forehead.

When they were both breathing more normally and calmly, Keri muttered warningly, "Don't you *dare* say you wish you hadn't done that!"

She felt the chuckle reverberate in his chest. "I'm not only glad I did it, Keri, darling, I *meant* to do it!" He hugged her and then eased his tight hold on her reluctantly as he continued. "I've thought of little else since I left you last night. I'm afraid Señor Villarreal found me woefully abstracted. He had to call me to attention several times and I wasn't able to work up much enthusiasm for the forestry products combine he was trying to convince me to invest in."

Keri couldn't resist. "Oh," she said guilelessly. "Are you branching out into lumber now?" and batted her eyelashes frantically at him.

He groaned in a satisfactory manner and she patted the arm which was still clasped around her waist. "I'm sorry, but it was only a very small pun," she said contritely.

"Those are the worst kind," he said darkly. "I hope you're not going to turn out to be an inveterate punner. It might put a tremendous strain on our relationship."

"Only when the opportunity is so irresistible," she reassured him. What she really wanted to say was *and what is our relationship?* but she couldn't put it into words. With her surrender to the urgency of his kiss, Keri had finally admitted to herself that she didn't want to continue to combat her growing attraction to Dain. No, call it by its right name, she admitted almost sadly. She loved him!

She had to accept the fact that he might only feel desire for her, but she'd just have to take that chance. She had run safe all of her life, but it had been easy to do. No man had ever attracted or affected her as Dain did, and she was now forced to reexamine the values that guided her life.

It all came down to the fact that she was going to have to take a chance. If she ran away from him via a job of Charles's finagling, she might be passing up the most important relationship of her life. Conversely, however, she might, and it was all too possible, be setting herself up for the most devastating and destructive experience she could conceive of.

She sensed depths in Dain, the potential for a deep and enduring relationship, but did she touch those depths or merely wade in the shallows of physical desire? That he desired her was evident. That he had desired (and taken what he desired) other women before her was also evident. She was not jealous of what had gone before, but she was fearful of what would come after.

Well, life never fit itself tidily into neat little boxes and if you tried to shove it into a too small box, you suffocated it. Life was for living and learning and she could only hope that the lessons wouldn't cost her more than she could afford to pay.

"Keri?" Dain shook her slightly to bring her wandering attention back. "What are you thinking about?"

Keri leaned her head into his chest. "Must I be thinking? Could I not just be enjoying?" She avoided answering him. There were some things she could not yet say to him. When she could say freely to him all that came to her mind, then . . . *then* she would know what price life would require from her. She pulled herself from his arms, and as she did so, heard and felt the crack of a pencil as her foot snapped it in half. It seemed she was fated to drop everything whenever Dain decided to kiss her.

She knelt and gathered up her steno pad and the scattered pencils, those still whole and the broken pieces of the one she had trod upon. Dain took the broken pieces from her and tossed them into a nearby wastebasket.

"You didn't really think I wanted to dictate a letter, did you?" he teased her gently.

"Well . . . no," she admitted, "but I thought I ought to be prepared for any eventuality."

"And were you prepared?" he asked with great interest.

She gave him a huffy look and he laughed. "All I can say is that if you were unprepared, you rose magnificently to the occasion. The mind boggles at what you could do if you were prepared!" He continued. "I want to talk to you, Keri."

She rolled her eyes heavenward. "I've heard *that* before!"

"Keri," he said warningly.

Keri composed her face into a reasonable facsimile of the prim expression she had cultivated as Miss Dalton and folded her hands before her. "Of course, Mr. Randolph. You were saying, Mr. Randolph?"

Dain laughed helplessly. "I've created a monster." He raised his hands in mock surrender. "All right, Keri. Honors even." He punctiliously escorted her to a chair by the side of his desk before seating himself at his own.

"I have to go to New York for two days. I'll catch the evening owl tonight and come back on the early bird Friday morning. I have tickets for Wolf Trap for us for Friday night. The National Symphony is having an all-Tchaikovsky presentation, and I noticed last night that you seem to favor him, judging from your music collection." He waited for her reaction. He was never quite sure just *how* Keri was going to react to any given situation. Would she acquiesce without an argument?

She surprised him yet again. "Oh, I do enjoy Tchaikovsky. Do you know what selections will be featured? My favorite pieces are the Capriccio Italien and Romeo and Juliet. I've heard so much about Wolf Trap. Are we going to sit on the lawn with wine and a picnic hamper? I'll be glad to supply the hamper. I have a recipe for Chicken Teriyaki that's marvelous cold . . . ." She paused and looked at him expectantly.

Inwardly Keri was chuckling. From the surprised, but gratified, expression on Dain's face she judged that she hadn't expected her to agree to his highhanded usurpation

149

of her free time so readily. He had obviously been prepared to ride roughshod over any objections she might have put forth, much as Schyler thought he was doing when he phoned and announced that they had a date Saturday night. The difference was, she was going to let Dain get away with it because she wanted to go out with him. She wasn't going to let Schyler talk her into going out with him. If Dain didn't make plans for her Saturday as well as her Friday, then she would. However she arranged it, she wasn't going to be there when Schyler knocked on her door!

"Well, the tickets are for the covered seating, but I'm sure we can change them for lawn seating, if that's what you'd prefer," he agreed easily.

"Oh, yes," Keri enthused. "Would you like for me to call about changing the tickets? And may I supply the picnic? You can bring the wine," she offered generously.

"Okay, Keri. Chicken, you said? Sounds good. Just call the box office. The tickets are in my name and we'll pick them up that night. Are you going to see Charles and Mary this weekend?"

"No. That is, I hadn't planned to," Keri hedged, remembering that she might have to retreat to McLean to escape Schyler if nothing else was offered.

"Mmm. Have you done much sightseeing in downtown D.C. since you've been here? I thought we might spend the day dipping into the Smithsonian if you haven't made plans to go to the Lawsons'. Then I promise to take you someplace quiet for dinner where there's no dancing. After a day of walking on marble floors you'll not be in any shape to waltz and neither will I, for that matter." He grinned at her.

"I'd love to, Dain. Could we go to the Air and Space

Museum? I've heard that it's fascinating. I visited most of the others many times during the time Dad pulled Pentagon duty, but I haven't been in Washington since the Air and Space opened. I might as well warn you that I am indefatigable when it comes to museums and art exhibits. When Dad was stationed here before, I spent many weekends crossing and recrossing the Mall, going from one museum to another. Mother complained that she and Dad couldn't afford to keep me in shoes because I wore out so many pairs sightseeing."

"I can see I'll have to dig out my old hiking boots," Dain teased her. "The Air and Space it is. Sunday we'll do something quiet and nonphysical, or perhaps I should rephrase that. We'll do something which doesn't require walking." He winked wickedly at her.

Keri blushed. He certainly had expressive eyes. "Have you any further instructions for me today, Mr. Randolph?" she said in her most repressive, Miss Dalton-like accents, striving to keep the fountaining excitement which flared like a fireworks display from showing on her face or in her voice.

His face assumed an expression of pure mischief. "You can call Miss Barth and tell her that it's safe for her to come back." Then all teasing dropped from his manner and he added savagely, "But God help her if she opens her spiteful little mouth again!"

Dain left the office soon afterward and on the whole, Keri was glad to see him go, and to know that she would have a few days respite from his disturbing presence.

Keri had repaired the external damage to her appearance caused by Dain's impetuous lovemaking before Bridget saw her, but there must have been some lingering trace of passion in her sparkling eyes and softly full mouth, because Bridget looked at her sharply when Keri carried in the coffee from the canteen for the coffee break. There was a luminous, relaxed glow radiating from Keri which had been noticeably lacking before Dain came back to the office. Bridget wisely kept her own counsel, but it didn't stop her from worrying. Dain Randolph was no safe playmate for a sweet girl like Keri!

The next two days flowed smoothly for Keri, neither too fast nor too slowly. Elise came back to work the next day. Keri had called Elise, ostensibly to inquire after her health, and had subtly let Elise know that Dain wasn't going to be on the premises for several days. Elise took the hint and informed Keri in a subdued voice that her "flu" was better and she would return on the morrow. Keri said quietly that she was pleased to hear that Elise was recovered.

Elise came back to her old desk, but the balance of power had shifted and it stayed that way. Keri oversaw the division of the work now and she was scrupulously fair. Elise did more typing in the two days of Dain's absence than she usually did in a week. Even so, Keri still turned out nearly double the volume, piece for piece. She was faster and more accurate than Elise, but for the first time in a long time, Elise pulled her true weight.

Keri spoke to Dain several times on the phone while he was in New York, but although he asked specifically for her, there were no personal exchanges. He was brisk and crisp and instructions flowed from him in a racing freshet. It was a good thing his office was running more smoothly and efficiently, Keri thought with some humor, or they'd have had to bring in a fourth girl temporarily to help handle the directions for reports, studies, and background research. Keri had joked to Dain that it was time for him to acquire another company, but perhaps it was not going to be so much of a joke as she had thought.

When Dain returned on Friday he looked tired. Keri only caught glimpses of him during the morning. There seemed to be a steady stream of people going in and coming out of his office in groups of twos and threes, and Keri was seriously wondering whether Dain might not be too tired to go out in the evening after all. She wrestled with her conscience and lost. She supposed that she ought to ask him if he'd like to skip the concert.

For a while it looked as though she wasn't even going to get to speak to him, let alone carry on a conversation of more than two or three words. He went out in the early afternoon and returned to the office only just before five. Elise was watching the clock, much as Keri had done at the start of the week. Even Bridget gave the impression of a race horse straining at the starting gate. Weekenditis was affecting two-thirds of Dain's secretarial force.

Elise's voice came through the intercom. "Mr. Randolph wishes to see you in his office, Keri. He said to bring your book."

Keri gathered up her steno pad and some pencils with a strong sense of déjà vu. She said good night absently to Bridget and tossed another good night to Elise, who was departing the premises with all speed as Keri started to open the inner door leading to Dain's office.

When she entered the office her gaze went expectantly to Dain's desk. He wasn't sitting behind it as she had expected, and she took another step into the room automatically. A hand came out from somewhere behind and to the left of her, firmly closing the door. With a reflex action, Keri tossed her pad and pencils out of harm's way—no sense breaking perfectly good pencils—and turned into Dain's arms with graceful naturalness.

He gathered her hard against him and this time he didn't have to tantalize her lips to yield their sweetness to his probing mouth. After the first long kiss he whispered, "Anticipation of this moment got me through two days of hell in New York." He kissed her again and Keri responded enthusiastically.

When they surfaced for air again, Keri lifted a hand to smooth the tired creases at the corners of his eyes. "You look so tired, Dain," she whispered. "Didn't you sleep at all while you were in New York?"

"Not much," he admitted, touched by her concern. "I got through four days' work in two so I'd be free this weekend." She recognized the look in his eyes now. "But when I did sleep, I had some very interesting dreams," he assured her wickedly.

Keri buried her head in his chest and was sure he could feel the heat in her cheeks all the way through his vest and shirt. "Dain!" she choked out in admonition and remonstrance.

He sighed and released her regretfully from his arms. "If we're to be ready in time, I guess we'd better go. I just wanted to tell you I'll be by for you at a quarter to seven tonight. Pack double rations in that basket. I missed lunch."

"Oh, Dain, are you sure you want to go tonight?"

He stiffened. "And what's that supposed to mean?"

She saw that he had misunderstood and hurried to explain more clearly. "I mean that you're so tired. We . . . we could forget about tonight and you could get a good night's rest." The concern in her face as she looked up into his was more convincing than all her words.

154

He dropped a swift kiss on her forehead and assured her, "Believe me, sweetheart, if I don't get to spend this evening with you, I won't be helped by a good night's sleep. My temper hasn't been the best the past two days. It'll take the New York operation some time to recover from my descent on them, and the only thing that made me even bearable was that I got to talk to you once or twice."

"Liar," she chuckled. "You could have been talking to Bridget for all you said. 'Miss Dalton, see that the Carlin report is sent directly to Ravenson's at once.'" She mimicked one of his conversations with her.

"The switchboard operators eavesdrop," he informed her, "and you were the one who said she wanted to be called Miss Dalton." He growled deep in his throat.

"I think I'd better go home and raid my refrigerator," she informed him. "I can *tell* you missed lunch. I should have cooked another package of drumsticks. No sleep, no food . . . you'll be a mere shadow of your former self." She neatly evaded his arms and whisked out of his office, leaving her secretarial accoutrements still scattered over his floor. "See you at a quarter to, Dain," she called back over her shoulder as she snatched up her purse and fled, laughing.

Keri drove home humming. She hummed in the shower and she hummed as she packed the picnic hamper. There were over a dozen plump drumsticks. In spite of her words to Dain, there would certainly be enough food! There were also crisp fresh vegetable sticks and rounds to dunk into a creamy cheese and wine dip and small cherry tomatoes just the right size to pop into one's own or another's mouth. Homemade onion and dill rolls which would still be warm from the oven were packed carefully in an in sulated container. Hardboiled eggs, already peeled, and honey butter for the rolls were fitted into odd corners, and frosted sherried fudge squares for a possible sweet tooth or empty niche rested carefully atop the whole.

Keri prepared herself as carefully as she had prepared the food hamper. She chose a comfortable but elegant golden brown pants suit, teaming it with a ruffled silk blouse whose first button was situated just where the second button of other blouses usually began. She was living dangerously but she was suddenly heedless of consequences. Charmé breathed fragrance at the pulse spots and between her breasts, her hair was softly piled atop her head, and a warm, soft, expectant look glowed in her eyes. Keri was ready. Her eyes were huge and dreamy and when the doorbell pealed, a happy smile curved her full lips.

A momentary caution made her glance through the newly installed peephole. How appalling to open the door to an unexpected and unwelcome Schyler! But it was Dain, recognizable, though distorted, through the fish-eye of the lens, who waited none too patiently outside her door. As her hand reached for the deadbolt lock, the door chimes pealed impatiently once more.

Keri whisked open the door and happily accepted Dain's kiss. Lipstick was replaceable after all.

"Mmm. You smell good enough to eat," he murmured softly as he nuzzled at her throat, moving down closer to the enticing, sweet-scented opening of her blouse.

"We are going to Wolf Trap," she informed him as she lithely evaded his lightly encircling arms. She shoved the hamper into them and he grunted at the weight. He hefted it consideringly and cocked an eyebrow at her.

"Must have been a two-hundred-pound chicken," he declared.

"You said you were hungry," she explained and picked up her purse. "I know I am. Chicken and Tchaikovsky . . . a natural duo."

They exited from the Dulles access road with the others who were bound for the same entertainment. Dain drove slowly through the housing development which lined Wolf Trap Road, keeping a wary eye out for late-playing children.

"I sure wouldn't want a house here," Keri commented. "What a nuisance to have periodic traffic jams right outside your front door all summer. I understand that there are daytime activities as well as evening performances."

"Yes, there's a children's theater and other festivals that are featured throughout the summer, as well as workshops in the various performing arts. RanCo is a supporting patron, in fact."

Dain parked the car in the rapidly filling lot, and with Keri burdened by the thick comforter and the wine bottle she carried cradled in her arms and Dain managing the hamper and the two collapsible backrests, they started the walk up the hill to the amphitheater.

They staked out their own piece of the grassy hillside by spreading the comforter Dain had supplied. While Keri unpacked and spread the contents of the hamper, Dain dealt with the wine.

Keri waggled a plate at Dain. "Something of everything?"

He grinned. "Just put my second helping right next to my first." He opened his mouth for the celery stick Keri had loaded with the cheese dip and she popped it in, neatly avoiding his snapping teeth.

"Never bite the hand that feeds you," she admonished

him sternly and handed him a drumstick to tide him over until she finished filling his plate.

The hum of conversation and the spasmodic notes from the orchestra as the instruments were tuned to perfect pitch formed an undistracting background for their meal. Keri was glad to see that some of the tired lines around Dain's eyes had faded and when he finally leaned against the backrest with a sigh of repletion, she regarded the pile of denuded drumsticks stacked tidily on his plate with some awe. He had eaten as though he'd not only missed lunch but breakfast and dinner the night before as well.

"Keri, I'd marry you for your cooking alone," Dain said lazily. "This makes twice that you've saved me from imminent starvation."

Keri was momentarily silent. Her heart had lurched alarmingly when he had tossed out that casual remark and she didn't trust her voice yet. She had realized, agonizingly, that she would like nothing more than to be married to Dain Randolph. She also rated her chances of such an event coming to pass as slim to none!

She finished packing the remains of their meal neatly in the hamper and asked him steadily, "Do you want any more wine right now, before I recork the bottle?"

"I must say, you take it calmly," Dain said mildly, but there was a lurking twinkle deep in his eyes.

Keri looked at him in bewilderment. "Take what calmly? Your poor dietary habits? I've never lost a boss to starvation yet."

"Well, he observed, "I've never asked anyone to marry me before, but I had envisioned a somewhat more enthusiastic reaction when I finally did. Do you think I'll keep you chained in the kitchen, whipping up gargantuan meals round the clock? Is that why you're not interested?

Believe me, my dear"—he twirled an imaginary mustache —"if I chain you anywhere, it won't be in the *kitchen!*"

Keri swallowed around a large obstruction which had suddenly lodged itself in her throat. She thought it was probably her heart. "D-Dain?" she squeaked on a rising note.

Dain was suddenly serious. He caught her hands in his warm, strong clasp and looked fully into her eyes. "I love you, Keri. Please marry me."

To the delight of the interested people on blankets spread near them, Keri launched herself into Dain's arms with all of the enthusiasm he could possibly desire. The kiss exploded between them like a fireball and when they finally reeled apart, gasping for air, they were given a round of applause. Neither Keri nor Dain took the slightest notice of their audience.

"I take it that meant yes," Dain said rather huskily.

Keri blushed but managed enough spirit to say, "Well, would you believe it was a positive maybe?" He reached for her again and she fell against him, laughing. "I didn't think you'd believe it," she said with satisfaction. "Yes, yes, yes! I love you, Dain. I'll marry you."

That earned her another kiss, as inflammatory as the last. Keri vaguely thought she heard the roaring of surf at the beach, but realized at last that it was merely the applause greeting the appearance of the conductor. The program was about to begin. The opening bars of the music sounded just like Mendelssohn's Wedding March, but she admitted fairly that right now probably everything would sound like the Wedding March!

Dain arranged the two backrests side by side and Keri settled snugly into the shelter of his near arm. He reached across and captured her hand with his free hand and held it warmly. Keri was in heaven and it wasn't the magnificent music that had wafted her there.

If the truth be told, until she looked at the program at the intermission she had no idea what selections had been performed. It could have been a jug and bottle band playing for all the attention she gave it. Dain loved her. He wanted to marry her. No music in the world, even were it sung by full angelic chorus, could compete with that fact.

They shared a glass of wine at the break, draining the last of the bottle Dain had brought. Keri also fed Dain fudge squares until he sighed, satiated. "Do you think you'll be able to hold out until breakfast, darling?" she asked him solicitously. "I think there's one more hard-boiled egg. You could tuck it under your pillow tonight for a midnight snack."

"Hush, woman. I'm building up my inner resources. I'm sure marriage must require a lot of strength, especially marriage to you."

"Is that a compliment?" she asked suspiciously.

"Ask me again on our wedding night," he whispered, "or better yet, the next morning." He lifted her hand to his mouth and she felt the tip of his tongue caressing the center of her sensitive palm. Fortunately the interval was over and the concert started again. Keri's breathing returned to what passed for normal sometime during the second piece.

They were in no hurry to reach the car, or to join the line of cars snaking out of the parking lot amid slow motion clouds of dust. Their stroll back to the parked car was delayed whenever Keri stopped to admire the star-sprinkled sky or when Dain stopped Keri to give her a gentle kiss. It was a slow walk.

160

When they finally reached the car, the parking lot was already more than half empty and cars were revving impatiently in line, waiting for their turn. Dain put all the impedimenta away, helped Keri into the front seat and joined her from his side of the car. In the darkness and privacy of the car interior Dain pulled her into his arms with a hunger that was well matched by Keri's own.

He ran his hands over her shoulders, down her upper arms, and over to her rib cage. The silky soft blouse was no barrier to his delight in the fullness which filled and overflowed his palms. "Mine, you're mine now, Keri. All mine, only mine," he murmured before he took her mouth in an almost punishing kiss.

It was with a distinct effort that he pulled himself away. "Never the time nor the place," he said wryly. The parking lot was nearly deserted and it was time for them to go as well. Keri snuggled close to him, sliding her shoulder behind his right arm so that they were close, but he could drive unimpeded. Daringly she laid her left hand on the top of his thigh, enjoying the feel of the flexing power of his leg muscles as he accelerated and braked. His hand dropped down briefly to squeeze hers and to press it more firmly onto his leg.

The drive to her apartment was swift. Traffic was light on the Beltway and Dain was a steady, skillful driver. Nevertheless Keri was drooping by the time they reached the visitors' parking spaces in front of her apartment. The wine, the hard week, and most of all, the emotions she had experienced, despair and delight, all took their toll.

Dain leaned forward to shut off the ignition and as he looked back at Keri, he caught her in the midst of a massive yawn. The yawn reflex caught up with him too, and he smothered one with his hand and then wearily rubbed the back of his neck. Keri grinned sleepily at him and he leaned forward to kiss the tip of her nose. "Come on, sweetheart. Time for all big-eyed little girls to go inside."

Keri agreed without argument. Her eyelids felt grainy with tiredness and she was fighting a losing battle against another yawn. Dain helped her from the car and tucked her beneath his arm. She slid an arm around his waist. He was so warm and so nice to lean on. She drooped against him wearily. They were riding up in the elevator before she remembered the picnic basket.

"I'll bring it with me tomorrow, darling," Dain assured Keri. "You did say there was one more hardboiled egg, didn't you?"

"Maybe even a drumstick or two and some cherry tomatoes as well," she enumerated with a smile.

Keri gave Dain her key and he opened the door to her apartment. They stepped inside, but Dain didn't close the door behind him as she had expected. Keri looked up at him questioningly and he laid a fingertip on her lips.

"I'll be by for you about eight thirty tomorrow, Keri. You'll need a good night's sleep to be ready to tackle all those moon rocks and space capsules. And I'll need a good night's sleep to be able to keep up with you while you do it!" He pulled her into a hard embrace. "Sleep soft tonight, my darling, and dream of me." He kissed her thoroughly, handed back the key to her front door and added quietly, "I love you, beautiful Keri. Remember that tonight in your dreams."

She smiled mistily up at him. "I love you too, Dain. Come at eight and I'll feed you breakfast."

"Done," he accepted with alacrity and went out, closing the door behind him. Keri gazed unseeingly at the blank surface for a long time, a beatific smile curving her mouth. She loved. She was loved. No shadow of betrayal dimmed the fresh luminosity of this newly acknowledged love.

CHAPTER 8

Keri was up early the next morning. If Dain's appetite to date for her cooking was anything to go by, she'd better fix a farmhand's breakfast. She decided on huevos rancheros, hickory-smoked sausage rounds, and hot apple-bran muffins.

When the doorbell rang at precisely eight o'clock, the apartment was fragrant with the mingled odors. Keri met Dain at the door with a hot kiss and the promise of an even hotter cup of coffee, and her heart turned over with love as she saw the smile in his eyes. He looked fresh and well rested, much as Keri herself felt.

She had slept soundly during the night, going to bed with a smile on her mouth and waking with it still in place. She had showered and dressed carefully, but with speed, in comfortable slacks, a scallop-necked knitted top, and low-heeled walking shoes. She looked fresh and curvy and the happiness that bubbled and frothed to fill her whole skin gave her an unmistakable glow.

165

Dain eyed her with evident appreciation. After the first kiss he began to nibble lightly on her throat while his hands pressed her closer to his hard body. "You are delicious, my darling Keri," he murmured.

"Hungry again, Dain! All you think about is food, I do believe," she gurgled softly. Her own lips were busy somewhere in the region beneath his left ear. The faint tang of his aftershave mingled with the warm male smell of his skin was leading Keri to do a little nibbling of her own.

They might never have gotten around to breakfast if the buzzer of the oven timer hadn't gone off to announce that the muffins were done. As Keri pulled reluctantly away from Dain, he announced bitterly, "First phone bells and now even your oven timer is in league against me! Your apartment is going to give me a persecution complex. The sooner I get you out of here, the better."

He had followed her into the close confines of her kitchen as he spoke and she grinned at him while she lifted the hot tins from the oven. She upended them, one at a time, over an insulated wicker basket and the muffins dropped smartly out. Dain lifted one from the basket, juggling it deftly until it cooled enough for him to take an appreciative bite.

"And speaking of getting you out of here," he continued while she served his plate at the table, "when can we get married? Next weekend? Can your relatives gather that fast? You don't want a ten-bridesmaid wedding, do you?" he asked with unconcealed trepidation. "I love you enough to endure a morning coat, but I hope you love me enough not to ask it of me."

The hopeful, questioning inflection in his voice nearly convulsed her. "Could we compromise on eight?" She teased him and laughed delightedly at his expression. He chewed glumly on his eggs and she decided to put him out of his misery. "I don't know exactly how soon Mom and Dad and my brothers can get here. I'll have to call them, but I don't need even a one-bridesmaid wedding. All I need is you," she reassured him.

He heaved an ostentatious sigh of relief and reached into the pocket of his slacks. "For that correct answer, milady receives a prize." He casually unwrapped a twist of soft fabric and lifted out a beautiful, glittering diamond solitaire ring. Keri's mouth rounded in an *O* of delight and disbelief.

Dain tenderly lifted her left hand and slid the ring, with its fiery marquise-cut diamond, carefully down her finger. When it fit with a snug exactness, he kissed the knuckle of that finger and said with satisfaction, "And that's to come off only to slide a wedding band beneath it, and *that* just as soon as possible. You're mine only now, Keri, and this is my mark, my KEEP OFF sign."

There was a strongly possessive note in his voice which surprised Keri. Somehow she had the feeling that Dain was speaking more than just generally. She had not considered that Dain might be an abnormally possessive man. His reputation had certainly given no hint of such a facet to his character, but then she had a feeling that she and Dain would both be exploring uncharted territory. She'd certainly never been in love before and she doubted that Dain had either. If her own emotions were anything to judge by, she could comprehend feeling possessive. She personally was prepared to scratch the eyes out of any woman who so much as looked crosseyed at Dain!

The glass, steel, and stone Air and Space Museum was impressive, as were the exhibits contained therein. Keri did indeed see moon rocks and space capsules as well as

167

flying machines of an earlier era. She wandered entranced from exhibit to exhibit, listening attentively to each recorded explanation. Dain bought her a guidebook at the museum bookstore and she paged through it periodically, whenever she wanted fuller information or was trying to decide what they should see next.

Dain kept her hand firmly clasped in his own, but otherwise was content to let her wander where she wanted. He was aware of the many admiring glances Keri garnered, but they didn't seem to ruffle his composure, especially since Keri was sublimely unaware of any man save himself. The sparkling ring on her left hand and his proprietorial air were sufficient look-but-don't-touch signs.

By three o'clock Keri was tired of things mechanical. She smiled appealingly at Dain and said, "Could we go to the National Gallery for a little while? I'd very much like to visit the French galleries. There are some marvelous Impressionist paintings that I'd love to see again. My favorite ones are by Monet, of the Rouen cathedral at different times of day. The colors and changed light fascinate me. I could stand looking at the National Gallery's Rouen canvases for hours."

"Well, we don't have hours before closing time, but I imagine that there's time for you to at least renew acquaintance with the Monets. I gather that the National Gallery was one of your haunts in your younger museum days?"

"Oh, yes," she admitted readily. Then she added in tones of awe, "Do you know that the Gallery has a Da Vinci?" Her forehead wrinkled endearingly as she tried to express her thoughts clearly. "I think, over and above the artistic significance of the paintings, whether by Old Masters or not, they form, for me at least, a . . . a link between people long dead, touching me across space and time as nothing else can. The artist painted in his time and I see in mine and we are joined in a visual experience. The artist actually touched and made that painting. An author spins out the words, but the books themselves are once removed from the physical touch of the creator. For me a painting is a physical experience as well as an intellectual one.

"I felt that same link through time when I was in England. When I walked in the cathedrals, and even more so in the small Norman churches, I felt a kinship, a sure knowledge that others of my kind had walked as I did on those slabs, had touched the rough and dressed stone walls. We could have been walking side by side but separated by five hundred, a thousand years, those people and I. Does that sound too fanciful to you, Dain?" She looked seriously up into the thoughtful green eyes.

"No," he said slowly. "Not fanciful. Thought-provoking, perhaps, and perhaps a bit uncomfortable, but your ghosts must have been friendly ones."

"Oh, not ghosts," she disagreed. "Real people. I knew they were there even though I could neither see nor hear them." She shrugged and quoted Shelley's "Ode to Naples."

> I stood within the City disinterred;
> And heard the autumnal leaves like footfalls
> Of spirits passing through the streets . . .

"A tenuous awareness," Keri went on, "but neither friendly nor unfriendly. Just a link in the mind."

Dain took Keri to the National Gallery, as requested, and watched her lose herself in contemplation of the Monets. While she was absorbed, oblivious to his presence, he contemplated her. He suspected that she had a unique way

169

of looking at life and he wanted badly to understand her thought processes. Thought-provoking indeed.

She was still pensively quiet as they crossed back over the Potomac River into Virginia. She didn't question their destination, still immersed as she was in the slightly melancholy mood engendered by her mental meandering into the past.

Dain's apartment in Arlington was large and luxurious. Keri's apartment would have fit into it three times over. The carpets were thick and plush. Keri promptly took off her shoes and socks and wiggled her toes deep into the pile.

"Ahh . . . My arches thank you," she groaned. She looked around the living room with interest. There were deep suede cloth couches and chairs, comfortable but not impossible to get out of. Heavily textured fabric hung in floor-to-ceiling drapes and warmly oiled wood blended well with the earth-tone color scheme. Elegance and comfort were judiciously combined in a thoroughly masculine apartment.

Keri stretched out on the couch, much as Dain had at her apartment, and waved a hand lazily. "Don't mind me. I'll just inspect your ceiling while you whip up something tasty in the kitchen."

He gave a short crack of laughter. "If I tried to whip up something in the kitchen, I can pretty well guarantee that it wouldn't be all that tasty. Ham sandwiches, peanut butter and jelly, or scrambled eggs are about my speed."

"Do you mean that you brought me here to *starve?*" she wailed in mock indignation. "Or am I to rummage in your bachelor refrigerator and magically produce a six-course meal from a nub of cheddar cheese and the old rinds of bacon?"

"Fortunately we're both saved from that fate," he retorted. "My housekeeper had instructions to leave a meal ready for us. All we have to do is punch the appropriate buttons on the microwave and carry in the other food from the refrigerator. That is well within my capabilities," he announced with pride.

"My, my. How domesticated you are. I would never have suspected it," she enthused admiringly.

"Woman," he growled threateningly, "I am dangerous when I'm hungry. Get up and feed me."

Keri must not have been overly impressed because she didn't scramble up immediately and race into the kitchen. She got in one final word. "The way to your heart must be a superhighway, darling. You're always hungry. I thought love was supposed to make you pine and lose your appetite."

He leered at her and advanced toward the couch. "You, my proud beauty, give me appetites I didn't know I had!"

At those words Keri was off the couch in a flash, but she wasn't scuttling toward the kitchen. Instead she threw herself directly into Dain's arms. He lifted her and swung her exultantly around in a circle. When she came back to earth, they both went into the kitchen to see what Dain's Mrs. Babcock had left for them.

After a delicious meal Keri loaded the dishwasher. Dain protested, telling her to leave them for Mrs. Babcock, but Keri had elicited the information that the inestimable housekeeper didn't work on Sunday. Dain might be prepared to let the dishes sit in the sink until Monday morning, but Keri wasn't. She came to a clean kitchen. She'd leave one behind.

The apartment didn't have an open fireplace, but soft lights and even softer music set the mood well enough.

171

Keri curled up against Dain on the big comfortable couch, her glass of Amaretto and soda held lightly in her hand. Dain was sipping on a brandy, his feet propped on the wood and slate coffee table.

They talked about nothing in particular, pausing to listen whenever a snatch of music caught their attention. It seemed merely a natural extension of the peaceful rapport when Dain gently lifted Keri's half empty glass from her lax fingers and placed it beside his own on a side table.

He gathered her against himself and began to kiss her in a leisurely fashion, not aggressively, but quietly leading her into a mutual exploration of the sensory pleasures. She shared the taste of brandy from his breath and their tongues met and stroked in the soft duel for dominance which she gladly lost.

His hands were gentle but firm, sweeping down over her shoulders and back, to glide beneath her knitted top seeking the warm, smooth skin. The top was in the way, Keri thought lazily, and she never considered objecting when Dain lifted it over her head. He dealt with the front closure of her bra impatiently, fumbling only momentarily until he had mastered the mystery of the pressure needed to release the slide fastening.

He made a sound deep from the back of his throat and his hands came up to gently cup the rich flesh thus exposed to his pleasure. His fingers had a life of their own as they stroked and gently kneaded the firm curves, while his mouth nibbled and nipped its way from her lips, down the arch of her throat and onto the swollen mound his fingers lifted.

Keri was nearly frenzied from the sensations Dain caused. Her own hands were busy exploring the muscular roughness of his chest beneath his shirt. His body gave off heat like a furnace, burning against her flattened palms and stroking fingers wherever they touched the skin beneath the silky fur on his chest.

A shock, almost like a dart of pain, but without the sharp overtones, shot through Keri's body, radiating from the nipple Dain had captured in his lips. She felt his tongue rolling over and around the tip, felt the nipple swell into throbbing hardness. She couldn't suppress the low moan that rippled in the back of her throat, and when he began to suckle gently, drawing pleasure, giving pleasure such as she had never experienced, she whimpered.

"Honey, sweet honey," he murmured into the valley between the soft hills of her breasts. He lifted his head away from her enticing skin and pulled his own shirt off in one swift motion before he took her back in his arms and whispered, "I want you now, Keri. I want to taste and touch and know every inch of your lovely body. I want to place the seal of my body on yours as well as my ring on your finger. I need to know that you're mine alone now. I love you, Keri. Come to me."

The words were interspersed between drugging kisses and caresses, but Keri heard every word. He only put into audible words what Keri's body demanded of her. She pulled his head up to meet her avid mouth, giving him the answer he sought by the fervor of her kiss.

He said no more. He lifted her in his arms and carried her steadily out of the living room, through a dimly lit hall, and into his bedroom. With one hand he swept back the spread and upper sheet before lowering her onto the waiting bed. He gently removed the rest of her clothes before removing his own.

The kisses and caresses he had given her before were exciting, but now that he had the freedom of her body, he quickly enticed her onto a slow spiral upward to ecstasy. His mouth was fiery and as he sipped and feasted on the peaks of her breasts, she began to moan and writhe, pleading wordlessly for the final holocaust which would quench the flames racing through her body, in one final, splendrous immolation.

Dain worshiped her body with his mouth and hands, and when he covered her, spreading her thighs gently with his hands to take what was his alone, she clung to him desperately, her hands splayed over the bunched muscles of his back, digging in for purchase as he lifted her into his possession.

She muffled her cry against the smooth swell of his shoulder as the short, sharp pain ripped through her, and she felt him falter, hesitate . . . . She began to kiss his neck and throat and it was too late for his questions, too late for anything but the needs of their bodies.

When he could speak again, Dain lifted himself up on one elbow and switched on a shaded light. He turned back and looked down at Keri as she lay curled against his side. He gently brushed a rich tendril of hair back from her face, smoothing down the soft line of her cheek. Her eyes opened slowly, the pupils still dark and unfocused in the aftermath of her experience. She smiled, slowly, lovingly.

"My God, Keri," he said harshly. "You were a virgin." He sounded appalled.

Her smile deepened. "Yes, I *was,*" she purred, her voice throaty with satisfaction. She stretched and ran a hand lovingly through the hair on his chest.

He shot up in bed as though she had sunk claws into his skin. "Damn it, Keri, don't you understand? You were a *virgin!*"

"I know that, Dain. I always knew it," Keri said patiently. "What I don't understand is why it upsets you. I thought you'd be glad.

"Of course I'm glad," he nearly shouted. "I . . . I just didn't expect . . ." Concern darkened his face. "Did I . . . hurt you, sweetheart? I would have been gentler if I'd suspected, if I'd known . . ." He was floundering badly.

Keri was amused. The assured, sophisticated Dain Randolph at such a loss. She touched his face, his mouth, gently with her fingertips. "I love you, darling. You made me very happy. Are you sorry now?" she said softly.

"Sorry? God, no!" He gathered her into his arms fiercely. "I wanted you. I want you now. It's just that . . . well," he said awkwardly, "perhaps you would rather have waited until after we were married."

"Do you think we *could* have waited?" she asked wryly, her mouth curving into a wicked, woman-wise smile.

"No . . ." he groaned and began to kiss her desperately, hungrily, confirming his possession of her body again.

The next morning Keri wandered into the kitchen, wrapped in a short terrycloth robe of Dain's, to investigate the possibilities for breakfast. They had showered together, an exhilarating experience for Keri at least, and she had left Dain in the steamy bathroom trying to clear the mist from the mirror so that he could shave. She felt pleasantly domestic and just a bit stiff and sore as well. They hadn't slept much, but for a wedding night, as Keri considered it, it hadn't been bad at all. She stretched sinuously and the robe fell open . . . not bad at all!

She tied the robe again and started the coffee perking. She was very glad that she'd done the dishes the night before. How depressing to wake up to a sinkful of crusted plates after such a night.

She found bread, sausages, and eggs and laid them on

175

the countertop while she searched through the orderly ranks of pans for a skillet and the toaster. She had just found both items when she heard a sound from the direction of the living room. With a smile tilting the corners of her mouth she pulled the robe together again and walked into the living room, expecting to see Dain.

He wasn't there. She looked around in bewilderment. She was sure . . . she heard the sound again. Someone was rattling the doorknob and then she heard a key turning in the lock. The door started to open.

"Now, now you'll see!" There was a strident, vicious bite to the tones of the woman's voice.

Keri stood frozen, filled with a sense of horrible premonition as she automatically clutched the lapels of the robe together at the neck and stared toward the front door. Denise stepped out of the entry hall, into the living room, followed by . . . Schyler.

Denise caught sight of Keri at once and she said, jeeringly triumphant, throwing out an accusing hand toward Keri, "There, didn't I tell you? There she is, your precious Miss Dalton. She's my brother's mistress! I told him about her, and he came back from Europe especially, just to make sure she wouldn't be interested in marrying you, Schyler." She clutched at his arm possessively. "You're mine and Dain always gives me what I want." She laughed shrilly and said crudely, "Though this time it looks as though Brother Dear has gotten something for himself out of the deal as well. Play your cards right, Miss Dalton, and you might get some nice pieces of jewelry for yourself. Dain is very generous to his women. Something for everyone . . ."

Schyler's face was gray. He looked at Keri with anguished eyes and said painfully, "Oh, Keri, how could you? I wanted to marry you! You knew that. How could you do this?"

His face twisted into a mask of rage as he looked to the right of Keri. "Damn you, Randolph. She was *my* woman. I'll kill you for this." In spite of Denise's frantic clutch at his arm, Schyler lunged at Dain, who had come into the living room, unnoticed by Keri.

Dain was dressed only in slacks and there was a towel still draped around his neck. Traces of lather at the angle of his jaw indicated that he had heard the commotion as he finished shaving and had come to investigate.

When Schyler launched himself at Dain, Keri saw the whole sequence of events through a slow-motion haze of pain. Dain just had time to brace himself to take the shock of Schyler's assault. He slowed Schyler's charge with his left hand and drew back a strongly muscled right arm, cocked it behind his ear and unleashed the driving fist directly on the point of Schyler's jaw. Schyler dropped like a poleaxed steer. Dain sucked his knuckles and then shook his hand to resettle the bones into place.

"Now, would someone tell me what the bloody hell is going on?" he growled fiercely. "Denise," he said dangerously to his sister as she knelt by the prostrate Schyler, who was groggily rubbing his jaw, "just what the devil are you doing here in my apartment?" He nudged the recumbent Schyler with a disdainful toe. "And why did you bring him along?"

"I brought him to prove to him that Keri Dalton had no further use for him so that he'd agree to go ahead with our marriage." Her mouth quivered. "I think I'm pregnant and Schyler said he didn't care, that he was going to marry her anyway." Denise glared viciously at a white-faced Keri. "I told Schyler that she was your mistress, but

177

he wouldn't believe me, so I had to prove it to him. And I did!" she finished triumphantly.

Dain took a step toward Keri but stopped when she backed away from him, horror in her eyes. A muscle twitched and jumped along his jaw line and his mouth set in a cruel, hard slash.

Keri felt sick to her stomach, nausea rising in a bitter tide up her throat. She swallowed desperately. It was all horribly clear now. She had been conditioned by her godfather's expressed disbelief in her ability to carry off her masquerade of unattractiveness for any length of time, and by Schyler's easy recognition of her, so that Dain's seeming ability to pierce her absurd facade hadn't seemed suspicious.

Vanity had played its part as well. Because she had been so violently attracted to Dain from the beginning, she had been all too willing to accept the possibility that he could be attracted to her, despite her initial unprepossessing exterior and manner.

Keri clamped her teeth shut over bitter laughter. She was well served for any vanity now. Dain *hadn't* seen beneath her makeup and her frosty manner. He had known beforehand that she was not what she seemed. He had pursued her in a deliberate campaign because he saw her as a threat to Denise's happiness. The black irony must have all the old gods laughing now. Hubris in the best dramatic tradition, and her fall was going to be long and very, very painful. Something for everyone, indeed. The bill for her lessons in life was now due and payable and she was finding herself bankrupt.

She wasn't guarding her expression and Dain could read every painful thought. "Keri." He didn't appeal. He ordered and held out his hand toward her to enforce the order.

She looked at him and his demanding hand. Her face twisted, mirroring her bewilderment and sense of betrayal, her green eyes glittering with brimming tears. Keri was bleeding to death internally, lacerated by the glass-sharp words Denise had hurled at her unprotected heart.

"Dain?" she questioned him wretchedly, still hoping for a miraculous denial. "Is it true? You . . . you made me your secretary because of Schyler?"

"I'll explain later, Keri," he responded, neither affirming nor denying anything. His face was shuttered and she could read nothing except a proud demand that she trust him.

Dain's hand remained extended to her, rock steady, insistent, somehow pulling her toward his side with invisible ropes. He expected her to disregard Denise's words, to trust him before any explanation was made.

She had given him the gift of her body. Did that mean, on a cellular, bone, and blood-deep level, that she had also given him unwavering trust? She acted on instinct alone, because logic gave her no guidance. Almost beyond her conscious volition, she took an unsteady step toward him, impelled by the irresistible demand in his green eyes and by some faint, gasping hope she could not put a name to.

When Keri took that first step toward him, some invisible tension relaxed in Dain. The bunched muscle in his jaw smoothed. He watched her take two more hesitant steps and then he moved the rest of the way to her side. He lifted up her left hand, turned it over and laid a kiss in the palm.

He tilted up her chin and said softly, "Thank you, sweetheart. It will be all right. I promise you."

Schyler had climbed unsteadily to his feet and stood

179

swaying, a dark bruise already puffing his jaw. Denise tried to slip his arm over her shoulders but he shrugged her aside. "Keri," he said hoarsely, though it was obviously painful for him to form words, "Keri, I'll marry you still. I won't care about him. Don't you understand? You're my woman."

"Shut up, Van Metre," Dain snarled savagely. "She's not your woman. She was *never* your woman." He lifted Keri's hand and the blazing diamond scintillated with a life of its own. "She is *my* woman and she'll be my wife as soon as her parents arrive, or before then if she doesn't want to wait for them. If I ever catch you anywhere near Keri again, I'll break your neck. Now get out of here and take my bitch of a sister with you. What you do with her afterward is your business, but I want you both out of my apartment. Now!"

"But, Dain . . ." Denise wailed, no longer the haughty, beautiful woman. She was a scared, haggard woman whose spite had rebounded violently upon her own head. Dain watched her with implacable eyes, no mercy or liking visible on the closed mask of his face.

"Get out, Denise. I'll deal with you later." His voice was hard and unforgiving. He slid his arm around Keri's shaking shoulders, pulling her warmly against the strength of his body. He could feel her trembling violently, constant shudders rippling over her skin.

He turned her fully into his arms and bent protectively above her, holding her sheltered from sight of the other two as they departed. When they heard the sound of the door closing violently, Keri sagged limply against Dain. He caught her behind the shoulders and knees and lifted her into his arms. Her hand came up to touch the side of his neck as he walked over to the couch, where he sat down.

Keri cried. She couldn't help herself. Deep gasping sobs convulsed her and she gulped helplessly. Dain could feel her tears running down the side of his neck and onto his chest.

"Oh, honey, please don't cry. You tear me up inside when you do that," he pleaded softly, stroking the disheveled waves of her hair. He rocked her in his arms, murmuring soothing words. "Please, baby, please stop. You'll make yourself sick. I love you, Keri, honey. Please believe me."

Gradually Keri's sobs diminished to gasping hiccups and she snuffled wearily. "I don't have a handkerchief, honey. Sit here and I'll get you a washcloth," Dain said softly as he deposited her carefully on the couch. He came back moments later and began to wipe her tear-swollen face with a cold, damp washcloth. He also had brought a wad of tissues which he handed her. She blew her nose strongly and felt marginally better.

Dain took back the tissues and the washcloth, tossing them all on a counter in the kitchen. He came back into the living room, sat down by Keri, and put his arms around her, pulling her tightly against his side. She tried to stiffen, but he wouldn't allow it.

"All right, love," he said resignedly. "Let's get it over with, but before we start, I want you to remember this: I love you. I am going to marry you. Keep that in mind while we get over the heavy ground."

He looked savage again as he said, "I came in on the tail end of Denise's speech, where she offered you jewelry on my behalf. I can guess what came before, but maybe you'd

181

better tell me what she said so that I don't miss any salient points."

Keri drew in a shudderingly deep breath and replied obediently in a toneless voice. "She said that you came home from Europe to take me away from Schyler so that he would marry her instead of me. She said that you made me your mistress for the same reason. She said that you always give her what she wants, but that this time you got a little something for yourself as well. The rest you heard."

Dain's voice hissed sharply between his teeth and the curse he muttered not very inaudibly should have shocked her profoundly, but she was too numb to care. "It's mostly my fault, darling," he admitted heavily. "My father and I let her become the spoiled and spiteful bitch she is. I am guilty of that. I am guilty of coming back to the States early because of her call, but only because I was worried about her. She was hysterical the night she called me and she's unstable at times. I thought I'd better come home to be on hand. My father's not well and he's in no shape to deal with her in one of her moods." Keri didn't think anyone was capable of dealing with Denise in one of her moods if they were anything like what she'd already seen this morning.

"I also admit that I took you away from Simonds because I wanted to see you up close," Dain continued. "Any woman who could lure one of Denise's men away was bound to be worth seeing! Imagine my surprise when Miss Prim walked through the door and stood before me, judging me for daring to disrupt her well-ordered routine." He shook his head slightly. "Well, for your information, my routine hasn't been worth a damn since I first set eyes on you. First you were a mystery I had to solve and then you were the woman I wanted for my wife, even when I thought you'd belonged to Schyler first."

Keri jerked indignantly in his arms but he easily quelled her rebellion. "He told me you were his mistress, Keri," Dain explained hurriedly. "When he was explaining why he wanted to break his engagement to Denise he said definitely that you had been his mistress, that you'd quarreled and afterward you had left Van Metre's for parts unknown. He also said that now that he'd found you again, he wanted to marry you as he should have done before."

Dain continued. "The first night I called you at your home, before the conference, he was at your apartment. I heard you speaking to him. And then, when I came to pick you up before the reception, he called you on the phone. I had no reason to doubt what he'd said, Keri, but it didn't matter, or rather," he said with painful honesty, "it mattered, but I loved you too much to let you go. I'm not lily white myself"—here Keri choked slightly—"and I told myself that I had no right to expect more of you than I could offer." For the first time he forced her to look at him directly. "We start fresh from last night, darling. There's been no one since I met you. There'll be no one else for either of us from now on."

She didn't say anything—she couldn't. When the silence had stretched painfully long he ordered desperately, "Talk to me, Keri. Believe me!"

Keri didn't answer him directly. "I left Van Metre's because of Schyler," she told him quietly. "He hounded me at work and at home. He wouldn't take no for an answer, so I went to my aunt's for a while. Then I got Charles to arrange the job at RanCo so I wouldn't have to ask Van Metre's for a reference. I was afraid it would enable Schyler to track me down again. Then he saw me at RanCo. He started coming around and calling, just like before. I couldn't get him to believe that I didn't love him, wouldn't marry him. He just kept on and on. I didn't want him!" Her voice took on a perilous wobble.

Dain folded her tightly to himself and said bitterly, "If I'd known what a nuisance he's been making of himself, I'd have broken him into little pieces instead of just decking him."

Keri still hadn't commented on his recital, but she wasn't fighting his hold anymore. He had one more thing to say to her and then he would rest his case. "As for Denise and her aspirations, in the future she can fight her own battles, my darling. I fight only yours. I wanted you for myself and that's why I pursued you so relentlessly. Not for any other reason."

He waited calmly for her judgment. It wasn't long in coming.

"You once asked me for time, time in which to learn to trust you. I gave you that time, Dain. I learned to trust you. I still trust you. I love you too. Keri entwined her arms around his neck and lifted her mouth for his kiss.

His mouth swooped down on hers in a kiss of total possession. As he carried her back into the bedroom they had so recently vacated, he said huskily, "If your parents can't get back here within the next few days, Charles can give you away. You're not going back to that apartment either, except to pick up some clothes, and I defy the phone to ring while we're there."

"Yes, Mr. Randolph," she said submissively as he spread open the robe which was her only covering. His hands covered her breasts as she drew his head down to hers.

184

Keri didn't go back to her apartment, except to pick up some of her clothes, and Dain didn't go to work. Long distance phone calls established that Keri's parents couldn't be at the wedding if it were to be held in less than two weeks' time. Charles was pressed into service to give the bride away. Mary cried at the wedding, standing in, she tearfully announced, for the mother of the bride, who would have wept for joy had she been present. Dain's father attended and was patently pleased with the new addition to the family. Denise was not present. Keri didn't ask whether she had been invited.

Mrs. Babcock had duly tendered her congratulations, laid the table for the wedding dinner à deux, iced the champagne, and left. Dain said whimsically, "Dare I say 'Alone at last'?"

Keri chuckled. "*You* might dare. I certainly wouldn't. We've been alone, mostly, for the past three days. Are you sure we need a honeymoon?" She blushed violently as he whispered in her ear exactly why they needed a honeymoon.

He grinned odiously and kissed her hot cheek. "I didn't realize that you could still do that."

"Of course I can"—she glared at him—"if you say things like that to me!" A mischievous smile curled over her mouth. "Can we really do something like that? Marriage is going to be a lot more interesting than I had thought!"

Dain shouted with laughter.

Keri sobered suddenly. She leaned back against him and his hands came up to clasp loosely around her waist. She tilted her head sideways and looked up at him, her eyes serious and troubled. She really didn't want to talk about it, but she had to know.

"Darling," she began uncertainly, "what about Denise and Schyler?" She felt him stiffen and his hands tightened at her waist. She laid her own hands over his and hurried on. "Is she pregnant? And if she is, what are they going to do about it?"

He didn't answer her at once. She could feel the reluctance to discuss it in every hard line of his lithe body. He still hadn't forgiven Denise for her attack on Keri, but Keri knew that eventually he must. Denise was his sister and he felt responsible for her. If she were in trouble, they would have to be ready to help her as best they could.

Keri hadn't forgiven Denise either yet, but she had been responsible for bringing Keri and Dain together. Had it not been for Denise's machinations, Keri might still have been anonymously ensconced in Mr. Simonds's office. Keri was much happier where she was now, held closely against Dain's strong body. So she persisted.

"What are they going to do?" she repeated.

"She's pregnant," Dain answered heavily. "I talked to Schyler while you were at the beauty parlor this morning. He'll marry her, because his father wants an heir and because Schyler has no hope of getting you. It's a hell of a basis for a marriage, but at least the child will have a legal father. More than that can't be said for it."

His hands slid up from her waist to cup her breasts. He didn't want to talk or think about Denise and Schyler anymore!

"Don't you want some of Mrs. Babcock's dinner? She worked very hard." Keri was slightly breathless. Dain's hand had slipped inside of her dress and bra and was tracing circles around a nipple, rubbing lightly and tantalizingly.

"No."

"Do you want any . . . ohh . . . champagne?"

His other hand was undoing the buttons down the front of her dress.

"No."

The dress slid off her shoulders and dropped in a pool of frothy white at her feet. Dain unsnapped the catch of her bra and it followed her dress to the floor. He had finally mastered the intricacy of the slide fastening.

"No champagne?" she whispered as he picked her up and carried her into the bedroom.

"I'll drink it from your navel. Later." His mouth closed firmly over hers, silencing her questions. His hands were busy. He had learned how to take off clothes very quickly in the past three days. Sometimes he wondered why they'd been invented.

When his mouth left hers and went wandering lower, Keri discovered that she really didn't have any more questions to ask him. He was answering them all very comprehensively, in the most direct way possible.

He moved above her and she reached up to him eagerly. A very satisfactory basis for a marriage indeed.

LOOK FOR NEXT MONTH'S
CANDLELIGHT ECSTASY ROMANCES™:

Anne N. Reisser, a voracious reader, confesses a preference for writing novels to doing household chores. Although currently living in California with her family, she makes her hometown wherever she happens to be at the time—feeling that home is a state of mind and not necessarily a physical place. She is currently working on another Candlelight Ecstasy Romance™.

Love—the way you want it!

Candlelight Romances

Candlelight Ecstasy Romances

Dell Bestsellers